THE STREETS WILL TALK

Yolanda Moore

Lock Down Publications and Ca$h Presents

The Streets Will Talk

A Novel by *Yolanda Moore*

Yolanda Moore

Lock Down Publications
Po Box 944
Stockbridge, Ga 30281

Visit our website @
www.lockdownpublications.com

Lock Down Publications
Like our page on Facebook: Lock Down Publications @
www.facebook.com/lockdownpublications.ldp
Book interior design by: **Shawn Walker**
Edited by: **Kiera Northington**

Stay Connected with Us!

Text **LOCKDOWN** to 22828 to stay up-to-date with new releases, sneak peaks, contests and more…
Thank you.

Yolanda Moore

Submission Guideline.

Submit the first three chapters of your completed manuscript to ldpsubmissions@gmail.com, subject line: Your book's title. The manuscript must be in a .doc file and sent as an attachment. Document should be in Times New Roman, double spaced and in size 12 font. Also, provide your synopsis and full contact information. If sending multiple submissions, they must each be in a separate email.

Have a story but no way to send it electronically? You can still submit to LDP/Ca$h Presents. Send in the first three chapters, written or typed, of your completed manuscript to:

LDP: Submissions Dept
Po Box 944
Stockbridge, Ga 30281

DO NOT send original manuscript. Must be a duplicate.

Provide your synopsis and a cover letter containing your full contact information.

Thanks for considering LDP and Ca$h Presents.

Acknowledgements

I want to first thank my heavenly father for being so good to me, words can't even describe. Cash, thank you for accepting me into your family and allowing me to earn a seat at the LDP table. For my brothers and sisters who are also in the writing game, I'm encouraging you to keep pushing that pen! To my family, thanks for holding me down. Miracle and Nasir Moore, my beautiful kids, you make momma sooo proud and I just want to tell you I love you. Those words aren't enough for what I feel. Markal, Katrina, Latoya, Lakiva and Larry, I love y'all no matter what, and I hope one way or another I have been a good sister to you all. Devin Simon, my baby dad! You are awesome, thank you for raising a son to be man. Each year he grows, I know you are the water to our plant, thank you for holding me down. Adrienne, sis, *When A Good Girl Goes Bad*, check it out Adrienne Johnson. You have been my go-to person from day one and I want you to know when and if you'll ever need me, I will be there. I love you and no matter where life will take you, I promise to be right there with you. Ashley London, too many words to express what you mean to me and not enough ink but know that I got your front just like you got my back. You are definitely a sister from another mother but in our situation, blood means nothing compared to what we have! Tell your hubby, Josh London, thanks for sharing you with me. Milton Fuller, even though I can't figure you out I'm trying, love you. Myke, you know I had to give you a shout-out you are encouraging me with, *Trap Rising Empire*. I'm proud, remember you can do anything you set out to do, you just gotta keep going when things seem too hard to obtain. With that said, I'ma encourage you to be good or good at it, love you. In closing, I'd like to give the people on lock in the state of Louisiana a shout-out. Things are changing and your time is coming. With God, all things are possible. Niketra De-louch, my bestie, I love you. Keep focused and remember what I told you, this place isn't the end. duh look at me on that real count down. Danielle Matherne, thanks for looking over my work and my bullshit, love ya. Danena Williams, it's al-most over girl, love you too. To my readers, I hope that you enjoyed *C.R.E.A.M 1* and *2*. Stand by for part *3*, it's coming soon and lastly, enjoy *The Streets Will Talk*.

Peace, love and sanity

Dedication

I would like to dedicate this book to my mom and dad, Sandra and Larry Moore, may you sleep in peace.

Yolanda Moore

Desire

I hate my life. I haven't always felt this way. I came from a decent family, a two-parent home and being the only child has rewarded me quite a bit in life. We lived a middle-class life and honestly, I can't look back and complain. I love my mother like a mother should be loved, but boy was I a daddy's girl. He has always treated me like the princess I have been groomed to be and everyone knew I was the apple of his eye. Which is one of the reasons I felt compelled to leave home and also how I ended up in the Southside Projects. I always knew from the start this wasn't the place for me but thinking with my heart and not my head, has landed me right smack dab in the middle of this roach and rat-infested prison.

Five years ago, I lost my mother to lung cancer and to this day it still hurts. Mom's death is still a mystery to me because one thing she didn't do was contaminate her lungs with cigarettes. She hated smoke and even though my father smoked like a freight train, he never enjoyed them in the comfort of our home. As I said, I just don't get it.

Now, back to my reason for leaving home and falling into the arms of a man I thought could afford me the love and affection my father once bestowed upon me. Yeah, that was until he remarried the wicked witch of the west. Eartha stormed right into our home and took a seat in what my mom had considered her throne for many, many years. I have always been a conservative person, but this was just some shit I couldn't comply with. However, approaching my father about this and what I thought at the time was a fling turned out very bad. That day, he broke my heart for the first time in life, giving me the bad news that he had thought about marriage.

"Well, fuck me!" I screamed, not being able to help myself as my small hand connected to the stubble he'd started to grow on his face.

I'd never in my life disrespected my father and never had he disrespected me either. That was until the day he let his fat bitch slap me without saying anything. He never allowed my own mother to lay hands on me, so it fucked me up to hear him say Eartha made a mistake and it was a reflex when she had hit me. Right game, wrong bitch.

That was the last day I laid eyes on my father and his two-faced bitch. What made the whole situation fucked up was the fact that Eartha was my mom's sister, and I would be damned if my aunt became my stepmother. I just wasn't up for entertaining that sick ass shit. *I know my poor mother is rolling around in her grave*, I thought, shaking my head. Anyway, I ran away from home in the hopes of finding love, looking for what my father used to give me at one point in my life. Yet here it is, five years and sometime later, and I am still searching.

I hadn't fallen in this trap by default, I stumbled up on the man I thought was the love of my life. Come to find out, I was wrong like a priest having sexual relations with little boys. Derrick was exactly the opposite of what I had perceived him to be. From the outside looking in, he was the perfect man for me, but trust me when I say the saying, "Never trust a book by its cover" is true. I should have read and studied his ass from start to finish, but by then it was too late, and my black ass had been black balled.

I was contagiously wasted in his sauce. His swag lit my fire but his description for keeping me going is what literally killed my soul and I hated that part of him. His ulterior motives were deadly and even though I knew all of this, I didn't care. I still held onto his leash. Why you ask? Because I'm his puppet. I'm attached to his strings, he controlled me. He told me when to kill, when to steal and when to destroy. He made me the devil, and my mind, body and soul had become his personal playground. I'm talking serious daddy issues, right? I knew I had to get ahold of myself, but I always questioned, did I really want to? Has getting myself together become a need? Or was it because of the gossip flowing around these darn projects that has gotten to me? Or was it the bitches that snickered every time I walked by like my shit didn't stink? Fuck what you heard, but I refuse to walk around here like anything else.

As I said, I come from a middle-class neighborhood and honestly didn't know shit about the trenches or the slums they rap about in these rap songs that's getting muthafuckas forty-to-life. Anyway, I couldn't distinguish if my emotional and physical state was life threatening because the dick had me wrapped and tied in a bow. The bottom line is his love is like no other. Even though I felt his love came with a price, I am willing to bet my last dollar he would keep me safe and warm, even if that meant I had to struggle at the end of the day.

Now don't get me wrong, some of the shit that goes down in the Southside Projects had a bitch ready to pack my shit and go running home to Daddy. I couldn't dare swallow my pride and bite the bullet. Shit hadn't gotten that bad just yet. As I was saying, it wasn't perfect and as soon as Derrick was running the streets, guess what? I was sick, lonely and depressed all over again. The list of his bullshit just went on and on. With that said and done, I did everything to keep him by my side, no questions asked.

He sometimes abused me mentally and emotionally, but the reason I stayed is because shit hadn't become physical. If anything, my girl a couple doors down, who we buy food stamps from, told me that I was actually abusing myself. I just let her words roll off my back like water rolls off of a fresh painted car. Who is she to tell me about my relationship, and she doesn't have a man of her own? Here it is since we've met, she always speaks of her prince in shiny armor and a bitch still hadn't met this figment of her imagination.

Every time her man is the topic of conversation, she can only tell me the nigga just left or he's too busy to come during business hours as if he had a job. What I meant by that is she has at least a rack of food stamps and was selling them bitches just to get by. How could she be fucking with a nigga that wasn't supporting her or these kids? Speaking of her ass, she's pregnant now but who am I to judge? I did make a joke one day about never seeing him in the daytime.

This nigga got to be a vampire because his ass always coming when the moon is out. "What's up with that?" I asked. To this day I still haven't gotten an answer but if she liked it, I loved it. Fuck it, we all had skeletons in our closet, right?

Anyway, back to him. My peace, my joy, my faithfulness, my centerpiece, my life, my world, my best friend all wrapped into one. I mean, I did lose everyone and everything around me except for Derrick and of course, let's not forget everyone in the Southside Project. Welcome to my freaking life!

Handsome, chocolate and strong is what used to run through my mind every morning when I woke up and went to bed each night. I used to think other women just didn't get the chance to ever find the love of their life. I used to live in a blissful dream each day, but like a tsunami, everything came crashing down like a big wave. Now I know the next question is, what happened and why I stayed, am I correct?

Well, real shit? Rumor has it that Derrick's been creeping around and even though I hadn't caught him in the act, deep down in my heart I could feel it. Just like my girl Meeka had a half of a man, whom I've never met by the way, I was damn

14

near in the same boat because each night I fell asleep alone, and the other side of the bed was always cold like ice. Derrick always tried to convince me none of it was true and that when he was out, he was making the bacon to bring it home to momma. So, with all of that said, I sat on my pretty little ass and waited for something to happen, because in the court of love he was innocent until proven guilty.

Yolanda Moore

Meeka

"Lord!" I shouted aloud, really praying that the Lord takes away this anxiety.

Here I am, six months pregnant. Pregnant again for the fourth time, with three different fathers. I would never admit that to no one else, even though it is what it is. I really need to get my life together. I called my friend Desire to see if she would mind watching my kids, while I went down to the public defender's office to see my court-appointed lawyer for a damn boosting charge I caught a few months ago. This was before I found out I was pregnant, of course. I am many things but to put my kids, born or unborn, in harm's way is not part of my character.

Back to how this here shit occurred. One day, I was on one of my get-money schemes boosting out of Dillard's, trying to supply the whole projects with Polo's and Levi jeans for the niggas. Dressing the hoes in rompers, coochie cutters and crop tops, and you know I can't forget the project babies. You name it and I was snatching it even off the display if need be. Every booster knows around the holidays and the start of the school year is when the most money is made, and I just wouldn't let the opportunity pass by to make ends meet.

I knew the moment I walked through what used to be a gate to enter the projects, muthafuckas would surround me like a swarm of bees to honey to get what I had. Muthafuckas knew what time it was when I came through. Half of the store price and they were gonna spend that money while the getting was good.

Anyway, to make a long story short, my ass was caught that day. Me and all the high price shit I had hit for. I was thrown in the parish jail and didn't know how the fuck I was going to make bail. I couldn't call my cousin who was babysitting to bail me out. Fuck, her ass was actually watching my kids for two 'fits because she had no money to cop her own shit. My momma was out of the question, because she was fighting a demon of her own. There were only two people left I could think of. They were, Ms. Ethel, the nosy old bitch of the project and Derrick, Desire's ole man, who I sell my food stamps to each month.

The first number I challenged was Ms. Ethel. She answered the phone on the first ring because of course she had nothing else to do but be in muthafucka's business, which right now was fine with me.

"Hello," her sweet little old voice came through the pay phone.

"Ms. Ethel, this me, Meeka. I got jammed up working," I said, waiting to see if she would bite my bait.

"Chile, all that stealing you be doing ain't working. I don't know what's wrong with you young people today."

"Look, Ms. Ethel, I need you."

"Need me? Oh, I get it, baby. Gone and bow your head so I can say a guide prayer for your safety inside those prison walls. Lord, please protect this dear sweet lost chile while inside the pen. Protect her Lord, from the murderers and sex offenders."

"Ms. Ethel!" I screamed, cutting her off, "no, I need you to go to the church and take up collection for my bail." Before I could finish my sentence, the old decrepit bitch hung up in my face.

Fuck it, one down, one to go. Derrick was now my only hope. I didn't hesitate calling his number, even though I know I'ma have to come off my fucking stamps for about a year to match what he's about to pay. Damn, fuck it though, it's a chance I'm willing to take.

Dialing Derrick's number took no time. My fingers clicked each button as fast as lightning bolts. I let the phone ring until I was notified that my call was either unanswered by fault or that the voicemail had come on. I knew he wouldn't answer, and I would have to dial him a few times before we would be connected.

"Thank you for using Securus, you may start your call now."

"Hello? Meeka? What the fuck you locked up for?" he asked while snickering as if this shit was funny, but knowing him, I knew he had to be smoking that loud. I instantly started craving what he was blowing. As if I had just hit that good, my lungs started to burn.

"Derrick, listen. I got knocked while boosting, as you can see the shit didn't play out how I needed it to." I waited to see what his response would be, but I could tell he was in the middle of puffing on the blunt because right after, he started coughing.

"Look, I'ma come through for you but you know you gone have to pay a nigga back, right? Ain't nothing over here for free, not even the dick," he said serious.

"Boy, I got you! You know a bitch good for it," I told him, not really knowing how the fuck I would repay him, but my mission was to get out that bitch.

"Aight, let me get that nigga Scrappy Doo, so he can sign the bond. You know a nigga can't get caught up trying bail yo ass out."

I knew he meant his girl Desire would be tripping if she knew he was bonding me out. Everybody in the projects know that Derrick was a no-good, dick-slanging-ass muthafucka. When I say muthafucka, I literally mean his big dick ass has damn near fucked everybody and they momma.

Coming back to the present, there was a knock at my door, letting me know Desire was here to watch my bad ass kids.

"Hey girl," I said, smiling stepping to the side so she could have room to step through the doorframe without my big ass stomach in the way.

"Hey," she said, smiling as my kids came running up to her as if she was the parent and I wasn't. I must admit she was good with my kids, and they love her just as much as she loves them. "So, what you think going to happen when you go see your lawyer?" she asked with genuine concern written on her face. You could tell she wasn't born and raised in the bricks, because bitches just didn't give a fuck about what was going on with you, only how they could beat you down to bring themselves up. Definitely cut from different cloth.

"Girl, honestly?" I took a seat on the couch, looking at the fake rose gold watch I stole. I had a few minutes before it was time to go. "I don't know. I doubt if I get time for this petty ass shit."

As for probation, even though I can deal with that more than being locked up for six months to a year, a bitch is tired of paying them muthafuckas. I'm damned near still on bench probation. I just pray God gives them eyes to see a bitch's struggle and not judge me like I'm just a bum bitch that would rather steal, fuck and collect government assistance.

"Speaking of," I, said, pulling my phone out. "I need for this damn PPP loan to hit my Go 2 bank accounts. Muthafuckin bills is way past due."

"Girl, we all in the same boat, but things will fall into place when the time is right. Trust me, it will."

"Bitch, fuck all that! I need my time to be right now, and it would be a big ole blessing if a couple of G's could fall right into my lap. That is the only place a bitch looking for something to fall. You the only bitch in the projects that keep water, lights and cable on at the same time. Bitches like me gotta choose what's more important," I said, looking with a stank look on my face, not because I was jelly of Desire. But fuck, I had to question God about this bitch. Like really, is she the only one in this muthafucka is being shown favor?

"Oh girl, please. If it wasn't for Derrick, I would have my ass right in the same shit."

"Not to throw in your face what you told me in confidence, but you don't have to live like this. What you need to do is get that thumb from so far up yo ass and start spending that fucking money yo daddy be sending your monthly, instead of depositing that shit in the bank to collect dust as if it's gone spend itself."

"That's something I'd rather not speak on."

"Alright, but bitch, you need to start being grateful instead of acting like a spoiled brat."

"You just don't understand," she said, and I could tell her bougie ass was in her feelings.

"Look, baby girl, a bitch don't understand that *Hallmark* shit you got going on. I know a father supposed to be the first man a girl learns to love, and he is meant to be her knight in shining armor, her hero. But I never met my sperm donor to even compare him to every man I meet. All a bitch know is to scope out the hottest baller, who don't mind spending money, and that's the only daddy a bitch like me has ever known."

By the time I complete my last words, I stand up and grab my purse, kiss my babies and head out the door to face whatever destruction there is in my near future.

Yolanda Moore

Derrick

I woke up to the smell of bacon, eggs and toast. I know that was my cue to get up out the bed. I must've fell asleep at my baby mom's last night when I came to lay the pipe down. Fucking her always made me wonder why I left her in the first place, but the more I think about it, it comes back to me and hits me like a flood all at once. Whenever she was on her knees was when we got along the best. Her nagging ass couldn't talk, but all in all, I kept coming back to this bitch for a reason. A nigga just couldn't shake that sweet pussy. So, whenever I did come through, I fucked her good. Real disrespectful like and pretended we were happy because on some shit, the things she did to me made me proud.

A nigga did love Desire, she is definitely wifey material. She just wasn't freaky enough for my taste. I don't mind being her teacher as long as she is willing to learn. Nigga know shit from sugar through being surrounded by gold digging ass bitches all my natural-born life. I can spot a gem from a mile away. Desire is the type of woman you bore children with, even though I have a team of them lil muthafuckas running round now. I can see my baby pregnant and barefoot.

After getting out the bed and washing up, I stepped into the neatly decorated kitchen. I knew Keisha had shit fit for a king. She made it a habit that we at least ate one home cooked meal together as a family, whether it be breakfast, lunch or dinner. Today it would be breakfast, because I couldn't miss the twins' first day of their last year of high school.

"D.J. and Derrion, come on and eat before y'all lil asses miss the bus," Keisha yelled as if they wouldn't hear her if she talked in a normal inside voice.

"Keisha, chill ma. Trust me, they not gone be late," I said, stepping into the kitchen while she stood over the stove.

23

Before I took a seat, I couldn't help but grab a handful of her ass. If you asked me, it was mine just as much as hers, the titties too. I paid for them shits and I swear on all the breath in my body, I would kill a nigga if he thought he could touch what's mine. I don't play that shit. Even though me and Keisha can't get along for too long under the same roof, she bet not let another nigga step foot in this bitch but Derrick Jr.

"Ma, you be cappin," my son said as soon as he stepped in this bitch, looking fresh to death. He stepped up behind his momma giving her a kiss on the cheek before he came and dapped me down.

"Boy, I'ma show yo grown ass capping if you miss that bus. You know I gotta open the salon on time, not be playing Uber for you and Derrion."

"Ma, that's something Pops will never put you in a situation to do. And as far you being late and not opening the salon on time, you own it. You can open that bit—"

"Watch your mouth before I make you wash it with soap."

"My bad, Ma, but as I was saying you can open it when you want."

"Son, you are so correct," she said smiling, "but time is money and if I opened the shop when I wanted, you wouldn't be around here acting like you going to a *GQ* photo shoot."

"D.J. M.O.B., lil nigga, be more like ya pops. I don't know where you get all that girlie shit from, always in the mirror and shit."

"Pop, don't no woman want they dude looking all trife-life. I'm staying fresh to get the ladies."

"Boy, don't nobody want a dumb uneducated thug." Derrion came down the steps looking like money as well.

"Aye, watch ya mouth, baby girl. I don't breed dummies."

"Sorry, Poppa," she said, passing Keisha, coming straight to me with puppy dog eyes.

"That's ok, baby girl." I accepted the kiss she planted on my cheek. As she took her seat, she stuck her tongue at her brother.

"D, you really acting like a four-year-old," he said as he got up from his seat to help his mom pass out breakfast.

"I'd rather act like a four-year-old than a bit."

"What the hell is wrong with y'all ass this morning?"

"Nothing, Ma, her Gorilla-Glue-head ass just mad because she knows Pops gone be gone as soon as we step out the door."

"Wait, wait, wait...you serious right now?" I asked both my kids. On some shit, it broke my heart to hear those words. "Come here, baby girl," I said as I pushed back from the table.

As soon as Derrion stood from her seat, my baby girl, my first born, collapsed in my arms soaking my shirt. I looked up at Keisha as she rolled her eyes at me.

"I told you, Derrick," was all she said when she finally took her seat at the table. For the longest, Keisha has been trying to get a nigga to come back home. But if I had to put my right hand on the Bible and speak the truth and nothing but the truth, I hadn't forgiven Keisha for cheating on a nigga when I was on lock. My pride wouldn't let me, not even for my kids. I told myself I didn't have to live here to be a father to my kids. I take care of all my seeds, the ones I know about anyway.

"Baby girl, look at me. Look at me, baby girl. You gone make Daddy cry too if you don't," I said, rubbing her back in small circles like we had to do to them both when they were babies. *Mane, how time has changed*, I thought just as she looked up at me with tear-filled eyes.

"If Poppa wasn't out making money, you wouldn't be able to live lavish. I know you like the way you live," I said, with a small smile on my face.

"I don't…like it…as…much as…I want you here," she struggled getting out.

"I'm sorry, my baby, that's the stupidest shit I could've said as if that shit matters to you."

"At least we knew you and D.J. have something in common, Poppa." We all laughed because we do be saying some crazy shit.

"Look, baby girl. I'ma do better, ok?"

"You promise?" she asked, holding her pinky out. I could feel Keisha's fucking eyes burning a hole in a nigga.

"I promise," I took her pinky, interlocking our fingers. "Let's go before y'all mom kill us all for being late. We will grab breakfast at Mickey D's or some shit, cool?"

"Cool," the three said all at once.

***

After seeing my kids off for their first day of school, I headed back to the projects to check in with Desire. I finally turned my phone back on and I was greeted with several missed calls from my wifey. If it wasn't one thing, it was another. Lately, it seems I need to work on the relationships with the women in my life. I been doing a whole lot of letting them down. I promised myself I would do better, especially after seeing the tears fall from my baby girl's eyes today. I would kill a nigga if they made her cry and here it was, I am the muthafucka who is causing her pain.

As soon as I pulled up to the projects, I took in the scene. *Even though a nigga hustle twenty-four-seven, three-sixty-five days of the year… I still haven't left this bitch*, I thought, shaking my head. Every time I tell myself it was nearing my time to exit the game, there was always more money to be made.

No lie, this shit is a fucking addiction and was hard as my dick get when I'm tryna bust a nut.

"Knock, knock, knock. Hey, man, you gone let me wash up your shit? Them rims looking kinda grim," Scrappy Doo asked as he stood there with his implements, ready to get to work. The nigga was the only muthafucka I know that live here, besides my girl, who had a clean record and good credit. Even though, this nigga did more dope than the local dope boy said.

"Yeah, you can wash my shit up," I said, stepping out my black big body Benz. "This muthafucka is my heart so if you scratch it, I'ma scratch that ass," I said, closing the door and throwing him my keys.

"Alright, African booty scratcher." This nigga had the nerve to laugh like shit was funny.

"Play with my shit if you want to, Scrappy and Ms. Ethel gone be down at the Lord's house, passing the collection plate around to bury yo ass."

"Mane, I got you," was the last thing he said as he took off in my shit, turning the system up bumping Kevin Gates', "Push It."

As I made my way through the stomping grounds that made me the gangsta I am today, I looked around at the little kids that were surely headed for destruction. It's sad, but like Pac said, "That's just the way it is." This shit around here was straight grimy. Mothers sucking dick to feed their kids. Niggas out here hustling to feed their egos, and all of us out here too busy with our own insecurities to even pay attention to the younger generation, feeding their anger with violence because we were too busy with doing what we thought was right. But how could we when we were never taught what's right? I feel my phone vibrate on my hip, bringing me out my thoughts. I wonder who is hitting me on my line.

"What's the deal, big homie?" I hear as soon as I pick up and I know it's that nigga Chris.

"Nothing, my nigga, just made it back to the slums. Why? What's good?"

"Mane, the police came through this bitch earlier yesterday evening but you were nowhere in sight, my nigga, shit went down."

"Thank God I wasn't at this bitch, because you know them boys in blue be on that straight bullshit when they spot niggas like me. Anyway, did anybody get popped?"

"Fuck no and that is exactly why I keep scolding these bird-brain-ass, wannabe hustlers to lay low. You know them pigs is laid somewhere in the cut, waiting for a nigga to slang their next piece of dope."

"Yeah, I hear that shit. I appreciate you looking out, giving me a head's up. You know I'ma lay low. I don't have to bump my head twice to know what should or shouldn't be done."

"A'ight, my nigga. I'm glad I could help out but look, I'm tryna get put on, ya heard me? You know shit been kinda rough since I opt out the pen."

Now I'm not a stupid nigga, I thought, but it's apparent Chris thought I was. His ass calls me, telling me 'bout the people coming through this bitch and not to make moves, because they were the wrong moves. But then, the nigga asked in the same sentence to throw him something.

"Look Chris, if you need a couple of dollas I got you, but you already know that's the only thing I'm willing to throw you. So, before the sun sets, I'ma come and holla at you!" I hung the phone up before the nigga could respond. I mean, I am not the type of nigga that will keep the next man down, especially when he own his ass, but I'm not a fool. Red flags were up the minute Chris' ass put police and dope in the same sentence. It only took me one fucking time to get locked up and so far, that has been my one and only time. Like I said, I wasn't the type of person that needed to see shit more than once. Usually, I always learn my lesson the first time, and didn't need to go through it repeatedly to have learned a lesson.

Yolanda Moore

The Street Will Talk

Ethel May Barringer

If I had the chance to start all over in a different world, with the rich white fold and a million bucks to go along with it, I would turn it all down just to be able to tell the story of the things I have seen coming and going out of these here old Southside Projects. I know and have seen plenty of things you wouldn't believe, even if you saw it with yo own eyes. Some days I even believe this here ole cataract be playing tricks on me.

The things I have seen I wouldn't dare repeat, because it could get you straight killed and thrown in the bottom of the Mississippi River, with cinder blocks cemented to your feet and tied with a bow. I know how to play my hand, especially when them blue and white boys come around pretending to protect and serve. Serve my ass on a silver platter, because the only thing them no-good muthafuckas been serving as of late is silver bullets. Excuse my language, but that is the truth, and we all know the truth sets you free.

These here projects have gone through many phases and with every generation, it ain't getting no better. It's always been about guns, sex, drugs and violence. Let me not even start on how they all tossing these different sexually transmitted diseases around. I don't want to even touch the topic about this white man's handmade drug, and these stupid mutha-fuckas running around here slanging the shit like they started some shit. But they don't even know the same people who taking it from them is the same ones giving them the drugs to kill they own people. All I have to say about that is, Lawd have mercy on each and every one of our lost souls.

I remember back in the day when the projects weren't the projects and were named, "The Southside Blessings," and boy wasn't they a blessing to many. Especially to us who hadn't had a safe place to reside when all that boycotting was going on I remember when we used to protest for all the right things in life like voting and drinking out of the same fountain as the white folk. Yeah, things of that nature. Now all you see is the young, black mothers protesting for more food stamps and for the government to build more housing to provide for Section 8 vouchers.

Even though things haven't gotten better around here, I still refuse to move. I would be damned if I let these lowlife, no-paying chile support, pant sagging, drug dealing, first-check-of-the-month snatching thugs run me from my neck of the woods. No ma'am, no Pam, no turkey. The only thing that could move me from sitting on my porch in my rocking chair is stray bullets and so far, the good Lawd has spared my life many times. and praise be to the Most High, I haven't had to dish out any bullets myself from my old friend Sally, aka Smith and Wesson. Back in my glory days I was something. You know what they say, once a gangsta always a gangsta, but that's a story for another time.

"Ms. Ethel May, how you, my girl?" I looked up and seen Keisha, Lawd help her.

Every time I blink my eyes, she is with chile. Half the projects done had her fast butt. She doesn't know I've seen all types of men running in and out her house, and I refuse to believe the high traffic was because of all them food stamps she was selling. It ain't that many food stamps in the world. She should be ashamed of herself, taking food out of a baby's mouth.

"Just out here soaking up this sun, baby, and praying over these here projects. Asking the good Lawd to heal and protect each and every one of you," I said, meaning every word that left my body.

"No disrespect, Ms. Ethel May, but you and I both know you been in these projects longer than any of us and ain't shit around here getting better."

It will get better if you stop opening them bony ass legs, I thought, but instead I said, "You can't expect for God's goodness to just fall into yo lap. We all gotta work together and I'm doing my part, chile. It's up to you younger ones to put the foolishness behind you, but it's up to you."

"Yeah, I hear you, Ms. Ethel. Excuse my French, but it's all bullshit to me. I'ma holla at you though. Keep me in yo prayers though. Hopefully one day some shit will change," she said, walking off but not before I got my last thought out.

So damn disrespectful. "I just seen that no-good baby daddy of yours pull up, maybe he can give you a financial break." I laughed under my breath because she thought no one seen her creeping at night, but I did. For eighty-seven years, these old eyes of mine never let me down.

"You got something for me, D?" I asked as I saw Derrick walking by like he was the man around here.

"I got you, Ms. Ethel May. As soon as Scrappy finish detailing my whip, I'ma send his package through you."

"Let me get you straight, because you already know you can't trust that son of mine with a stray dog, so you should know what I think about putting money in his hands," I said as I grabbed my walker to go get Derrick some money for my first-of-the-month medical supply.

"Ms. Ethel May, you already know yo money ain't good here. I'ma pop you off though," he said, trying to walk off.

"That is fine, my baby, but you know I gotta bless you with something. The era I come from, ain't shit free, so wait on the old lady for a few minutes," I said as I continued to slow roll on my walking. When I made it inside, I locked all three locks before I went to my stash. Before you judge me, let me explain. There is nothing in this world that could stop me from hustling.

Dr. Erica Faye has been prescribing me all kinds of medication for about ten years now, and the first time I took one of them ole blue tabs, Lawd knows it made me sick to the stomach and from that day on I never took another. I used to throw that crap in the trash, until I seen my son Scrappy Doo trading it for the ole crack cocaine, he be smoking off a can or a baby food jar. I knew then they had to be worth some money, because no way was somebody going to come up off that white mess if it wasn't worth it to them.

So, one day I sat out on my porch like I always do, and waited until I seen Derrick pass by, to see what he thought and that is how we started our little secret. He gave me weed and every time I tried to pay him, he would refuse and in return, give him a few of them little blue devils I refused to contaminate my body with. Finally making it back outside, I handed him the *Daily Bread*, I slipped the pills in.

"Make sure you look out for me now, my baby, but don't send it with my son, you know he not right."

"Ms. Ethel May, you know Scrappy don't smoke no weed."

"I know he don't, but just like he used to trade you my shit for that crack cocaine, he would find somebody to do the same with my weed. I brought his lil skinny ass in the world, and would surely take his butt out of this world with no problem," I said, holding up my brown bag special which is where I kept ole faithful Sally just in case.

"Aight, give me a lil minute and I'ma come back through and drop yo shit off myself." He began to walk off. "Oh, one thing for I bust out, what the fuck happen when I was gone?" I know he was talking 'bout the cops.

"That's boy Chris got jammed up, right along with a few of them other knuckleheads around here. Now, they let them all go, but I ain't no fool. I been on this earth long enough to know bullshit when I see it."

"What you mean?" he asked with his face all balled up.

"You better watch that boy who you call your friend. I had to learn that the hard way, when that witch Betty that stay on the other side of these projects, stole my Larry from me right from under my nose. Anyway, they had let everybody go and rode off with Chris and not even an hour later, they came back and took Demond to jail."

Derrick

That bitch Chris forgot to mention that and that's exactly why I wasn't fucking with his jail bird ass.

"Aight, Ms. Ethel. I'ma be back in a minute with yo shit," I said, walking off not even giving Ms. Ethel time to say nothing.

I knew exactly what had to be done. It's one thing for me to be taking penitentiary chances, but to let another nigga gamble with my life is on a whole 'nother fucking level. I gotta cake baked for that ass. I can't say I'm ever excited about getting on a nigga ass because I don't. Beefing gets in the way of making money, but I knew at times violence was the key with staying on top. And I had to admit, I didn't mind keeping my grass cut low to see where the snakes were slithering.

Fuck all that bullshit muthafuckas be talking about keeping your friends close and your enemies closer. I didn't have time watching myself and how I moved around a nigga. Fuck breaking bread with a nigga just to keep them close. If I'ma be breaking anything, it's gone be a nigga neck.

For now, I'ma drop by my girl and see how she coming. I definitely had to check her temp. I know I be fucking up a lot with her, but I hope she keep accepting the good and the bad. When I always walked inside our crib, Desire always had this bitch spotless, food cooking and she always served the pussy to a nigga on a platter. The people that knew me was probably wondering if Desire was my main girl, why the fuck I still had her in the projects and moved Keisha out.

I had my reasons, for one Keisha had my kids and I wanted them out this bullshit ass pace that had been my home. I refused to let them grow up here. Now, as for my baby Desire, I have plans on moving my boo up out of this trap. For the life of me, I can't understand why she stuck by a nigga side, but she did. Which is why I promised I was going to do just what I know she deserves.

"Desire? Bae? Where you at?" I asked, knowing she heard me. This bitch isn't that big to where she couldn't hear me fucking calling her. I guess her ignoring me answered my question she was mad at a nigga. As soon as I stepped inside of our bedroom, she laid on the bed in a red teddy, the one I loved to see her in and the one I loved taking off her.

"I know fucking well that book ain't that fucking good to where you didn't hear a nigga walk in, and then you got the nerve to be in here all sexy an shit."

"For your information, I did hear yo muthafuckin ass ask where I was. To answer your question, I'm always where yo ass needs to be, home in the fucking bed."

Damn, I guess the teddy wasn't for a nigga.

"Babe, I'm sorry. You know a nigga be out hustling, tryna get this fucking money to move yo sexy ass up out of here," I said, laying across the bed alongside her, sliding one of my legs between both of hers.

"Move, Derrick, I ain't fucking with you," she said, pushing me lightly.

"Why, you don't love a nigga no more?"

"Nigga don't give me a chance to love you," she said, putting the book face down on the page she was reading. Propping up on her elbow, she looked me in my eyes.

"Bae, shit gone get better, you gotta trust me. Don't you trust me? A nigga been grinding, tryna give you what you deserve, queen," I said, kissing her lips. I waited to see if she was gone kiss a nigga back to see what move I was gone go with.

If I know my bitch, how I think I know my bitch, then I know I'ma be beating that pussy up in no time. For one, she only wore this red teddy to make a nigga dick get hard and

38

that's exactly what was happening right now. My dick was 'bout to bust if she didn't let a nigga in.

Yolanda Moore

Desire

When I got back from watching Keisha's kids, I came straight home, cleaned up, put a roast on slow cook and ran me a well-needed hot bath. Once I got out the tub, I rubbed a light scent of Bath & Body Works body cream all over my body, more for the moisture than the scent, and sprayed a little Vera Wang Princess on all the spots Derrick loved. He'd place his nose on the back of my neck, behind my hair and behind my knees because when he licked the kitty, I didn't need him tasting nothing extra besides my sweet nectar.

Yes, I was mad at his ass, but I knew he was gonna walk his sexy ass right in here begging and pleading, and my clit was gonna betray me and start thumping for him to wrap those juicy ass lips around her backstabbing, two-faced ass.

Just as I predicted, she had let me down and even though I was fighting it, I was ready to throw purple hearts and wave my white flag. Even though I knew Derrick loved when I wore this red teddy, and every time I put it on the nigga would take it off not too long after, my purpose was to show the nigga what he was missing. And wherever he stayed last night, the bitch ain't have shit on me. I'm not worried about no bitch, because I know how to treat my man in the bedroom, but Derrick always seemed to bruise a bitch ego.

"Are you serious right now?" I asked weakly.

"Yep," he replied, moving down to my breast. As soon as I felt his hot breath through my thin lace teddy, I could feel my nipples turn to concrete. He bit on them, sending pain through my body, but pleasure as well.

"I'ma fuck you up one day, I swear," I moaned and right then and there I knew I had been placed under his spell.

"Damn, bae, you don't have nothing on under this bitch?"

"No, for what?" You know I like to keep this pussy available for whenever you ready for it." He slipped his hands under for easy access.

"Fuck… girl, what you tryna do a nigga, huh?"

"I'm trying to show you that you got a good bitch at home, and no one is working with what I got, nigga."

"Trust, you already do that, lil momma. You wet-wet, damn, I thought you was mad at a nigga."

"Oh, I'm still mad, I never said my pussy was. Now eat," I commanded and when I tell you in two-point-five seconds, all that bullshit I was talking was thrown out the window.

Derrick has had that effect on me from the first day we met. The nigga definitely had the gift of gab. Once I came all over his face and he didn't miss a drop of my sweet cream, I was hardly through with his ass. If he thought I was stupid, he had another thing coming. I was definitely about to make his ass put in that work. I know the nigga was out fucking last night because he came in smelling like Irish Spring soap. The blue kind at that and I smelled his ass as soon as he opened the door to our home.

The low music I had playing in the background only set the mood for what we were about to do. "Can't Let It Show," by Tank always made my pussy wet. It's just something about that man's body and voice that made me want to do everything he sang about in his songs. Laying on my stomach as naked as the day I was born, ready for his touch, my heart was truly torn. As I said, I knew the type of nigga I was dealing with, but I stayed because Derrick has potential to do right. I just prayed the man would stop being my Mr. Wrong, because I really wasn't sure how much more I could take.

I could tell he was ready and willing to do what was needed to please me with his big strong hands, as I lay sightly trembling from the orgasm I just had. Even though he is ready to sexually take me to another world, truth be told, I was just as ready to touch, caress and explore every inch of him, just to show and prove none of them other bitches will never have nothing on Desire. Starting at my ankles, he rubbed something on me. Maybe the Bath & Body Works, all the way up to my ass cheeks, smacking me hard as fuck. First came the pain and then the pleasure, which made me suck in air. He bit the top of my ass and smacked it again, making me arch my back deeper than ever before.

"Keep that shit just like that and don't fucking move," I heard him demand from behind me and I didn't. I could tell by the words he spoke that he was serious, and my heart raced because I know that I was in for a treat.

He spread my legs as wide as they could go like I was laid out in the snow, creating a snow angel.

"Wait, I'll be right back," he said, and I did. A few seconds later, he came back laying between my legs, still in the same position from when he left. I was so fucking ready to get fucked and he was taking too long. So, to keep me going I slipped my manicured hand between my swollen lips and flicked my clit as it swelled even more. Fuck, it was as hard as a jewel.

As Derrick got comfortable back into the position he'd left, he moved my hand and I could feel his tongue glide across my clit with a piece of ice, then slipping it inside of my hot box. Instantly, it melted. He sucked the melted ice out of me like he was drinking water out of a straw. Locking on my clit again like a pit bull in a match he was definitely winning, I felt him slip his thumb in my back door.

"Mmmm, Derrick, please fuck me. Ooohh shit, please don't make me beg," I said, throwing my ass back on his thumb as the friction from his tongue rubbing on my clit sent fire shooting up my spine.

"Mmuh. Tell me who this pussy belongs to?" he asked, and I was almost ready to give in, but I'm still mad at his ass.

"Fuck all that, just fuck me!"

"Oh, really? You trying to be a bad girl, huh?" he said as he flicked his tongue with precision.

"Oh, God."

"Who pussy is this?" he asked again, thumb fucking me harder.

"Fuccccck, it's yoursss," I cried out just that quick, tapping out. Lawd! This man knows not what he does! It wasn't even raining outside, but right in my bed we had just created a thunderstorm.

I'm moaning and speaking in tongues. I don't fight it because this is just what my body needs. Moving up my body his lips met the nape of my neck, as he found my gushy middle by sliding his rod up and down my split. He had no problem with pushing himself inside. For one, I was now soaking wet, which should be against the law, and I also fit him like glove. He trained my kitty for him and him only, and I hated the effect his ass had on me.

Not really in the mood to continue being the prey, I roll over on my back because now my body has a mind of its own. As if I'm under a spell, I look at Derrick with lust-filled eyes, ready to show him I'm grown. Without saying a word, my body is saying all I need him to know. I look at his dick as it greets my face coated with my juices, I take a handful and I run my tongue across the mushroom, licking the precum and my residue form his pole.

As my soft French manicured hand is wrapped firmly around his shaft, I suck and spit, suck and spit and suck, committing my sexual sin that I know to him is heavenly. I sucked the dick so beautifully that I could feel him shiver as if a chill had come through from NY. That let me know I was doing my job and doing it well. He gripped my head and started pumping as if he was on a mission. I knew he was about to cum and there was no way he was about to spare me. I ran my tongue up his shaft, then deep throated him once more. Just to add the cherry on top and to let this nigga know home is where the heart is, or shall I say the boss bitch, and that no matter how far he ventures off he will never find another me.

Keeping his dick in my mouth, I lifted his balls, running my tongue across that thin piece of meat without taking his dick out of my throat. Without warning, he shot his hot cum down my throat and I swear if I was thirsty, he had just quenched my thirst. I didn't let a drop go to waste. If I hadn't earned my crown any other time, I knew this time I had definitely taken my seat on the throne. Can you say, throat baby? Hands down, I had to give myself a round of applause and a pat on the back. His ass rolled over and slept like a baby.

Yolanda Moore

Jo Jo

"Ok," I whispered quietly to the bank teller, "this is how we are going to do this." I slid a sack over to the older white woman who I could clearly see shaking in her boots. "I need you to fill this bag up with as much money as possible, and make sure there is nothing but hundreds and again, as many as possible. Make sure there is no blue ink and if you press that button to alert the cops, I will press my button to blow your brains out. Do we have a clear understanding?" I asked, rambling orders out as calmly as I could, praying all went well.

She shook her head yes, which indicated she understood me. I let my words sink in to let her know this wasn't a joke, while also letting her see the print of the gun concealed under the coat I was carrying.

"Don't fuck with me, bitch, because I don't mind painting this glass or that back wall with blood and brains."

I needed this fucking money like I needed gravity to place my feet on solid ground. My life was in shambles, and I was on the verge of losing everything, not that I had much. I shook the thoughts out of my head, because this wasn't the time to become distracted and allow this situation to get out of control. "No time or space for slip-ups," is what I constantly told myself while I waited impatiently. It's a shame things got this hard for me and robbery is what I had to result to, but fuck it, life just isn't easy coming up in the Southside Projects.

"One more thing, make that shit fast," I whispered my last order out to her where no one else could hear me. I made sure to watch this bitch's every move. To be honest if she did make any false moves, the only option I truly had was to get the fuck out of Dodge. I hadn't really thought this shit all the way through and the fake gun I decided to use to stick up this mom-

and-pop cash checking spot wasn't gonna stop the rental cop from firing his shit at me. At least the muthafucker was old, so if need be, I could outrun his ass with no problem. I came out the womb running from muthafuckas on the other side of the law and would have no problem today.

My palms were sweating like crazy. I'm nervous as fuck, so the time seemed to be creeping, moving too slow for me. I tapped my fingers, waiting for the old white bitch to fill the bag with money. *Why is this bitch moving at a snail's pace when there is a gun pointed at her ass? Real or not.*

"Huh-hum!" I cleared my throat to let this hoe know time is money literally. I gave her a look that said, *bitch, hurry up!* As I looked up at the clock, she caught my drift and started moving like she knew what the fuck is at risk.

For some reason, I could feel eyes burning a hole in my back but was too afraid to look around and make things obvious. So, I just played it cool. I looked at my watch and then again at the wall clock as if it showed a different time. Life is a bitch, and it seems like I'm always getting the short end of the fucking stick, but it's time for me to be moving on up like *The Jeffersons.* And whatever it took, I was going to get a piece of the pie. I didn't give a damn if it was apple, peach, or pecan. I wanted my share.

I scoped this place out a little less than a month ago. I played with the thought, but never thought I would be this desperate in need. But today, I saw the perfect opportunity and when the right time came, I went with my move. I took the bull by its horns and rode that bad boy. Now here I am, with this cap pulled down to conceal my face, sweating and itching at the same time. I had no choice and the only option on the table was to get rich or die trying. Bills were overdue and if I didn't get this cash, I'd be on my ass out in the streets in the blink of an eye.

48

The old lady finally strolled her cripple-foot ass back to the counter with the bag filled with the cash as I commanded. *Good girl*, I thought. I smiled at her politely like she just cashed my check, and in a way she just did.

"Thank you so kindly, Judith, it was so nice doing business." I extended my hand for her to take, and she did with her nose turned up like I smelled like shit, and maybe to her I did but I didn't give a fuck, I got what I came for. I pulled her close to me and whispered, "By the way, if you do anything to get me caught up, don't think for one second I won't send the homies to follow you home. They will not only kill you, but your fucking cat will also get its head chopped off and stuffed in your mouth."

I pulled back, looking her in the eyes before I departed. I could tell I had her when I said her name. She looked spooked as a muthafucka. I had to laugh to myself as I strolled out that bitch the same way I entered, because she didn't even realize I read her name tag.

I strolled out the cash checking place with my head held high, but not to where the camera could see me. This place was run down, I doubt them bitches work. As soon as my feet hit the pavement, I walked as briskly as possible down the block until I reached my car. I wasn't worried about any other cameras placed on the outside either, because I had removed my plates. Not that them bitches were valid. Whenever it was safe to put them back on, I would. As for now, I needed to get the fuck on.

When my butt cheeks hit the seat, I came out of the hat I had on, placing my wig back on my head. No one will ever expect me to be the person behind the madness, because I never went anywhere without dressing in drag. Fuck no, wouldn't be caught dead. As I removed the shades I stole from the dollar store, I could finally breathe easy and look at the money in my lap.

"I did it!" I screamed. My thoughts were to count it right here, but the sirens in the distance told me otherwise. "Fuck you, Judith." I cranked my car and got the fuck on down.

I decided I needed a little privacy, so I headed to the Southside Motel. My home girl, Dirty Diana was nosy as fuck, so privacy is something I wouldn't get if I went home. She is a Spanish chick out of Fruit town I met few summers ago. We were both selling sex because we ain't have shit, but we took the little we both had and put it together and made it work.

She is also drag and proud of it. Her brothers were all she had, well used to have, until they disowned her and threw her out on her ass. She has told me many stories about how they used to beat her ass, thinking they could beat the faggot out of her. Shaking my head at the thoughts, *poor thing*. The beatings of course didn't work, so they had written her out of their lives, and she has been the sister I never had.

Even though I still fucked with my family and the same coming from them, Pastor John didn't have any understanding why his "son" wanted to be a woman. Like I told him, you can't pray the way I was born away. I told that nigga take it or leave it and of course, him being a God-fearing man has taught him to love no matter what, so even though his prayers are falling on deaf ears he still fucks with me. My mom wouldn't have it no other way.

I thought back to before my father became a pastor of his own church and we all lived in the projects. Shit was tough for a bitch. Roaches, no food, dirty clothes, you know the shit I'm talking about. A bitch was straight dusty-foot, but I have to admit that shit didn't stop a bitch from making ends meet. As long as I knew how to throw this good pussy, I'll never be broke. Of course, my parents always questioned me about how

I was getting all the fly shit I had, but I would always tell them my friend from school gave me his clothes. This was before I came out, and even though I didn't dress like a straight-out thug, I still kept it soft rocking my Polo shirts and cargo shorts.

If a muthafucka looked hard enough they would be able to see exactly what I was. I stayed getting my feet and hands done, but my parents looked over that fact, taking it as if I was just OCD. With all that shit said, when my father started bringing home the bacon, we moved out the projects to an upscale neighborhood with the rich white folks. When I tell you that was probably the worst thing that could've happened, well to my parents. I had been fucking and sucking everybody's husband that allowed my lips to bless them with what I was working with. And trust me when I say the shit wasn't free, I refused to fuck for free, for what? Yeah, my shit was that good.

Anyway, I ended up right back in the projects, because a bitch was well respected and every time I stepped out of my home, I didn't have to worry about being judged. Plus, you can take a bitch out the projects, but you can't take the projects out the bitch.

Coming out of my thoughts, I pushed it down North Street, trying to make it to my destination as quick as possible. Even though I was out of sight my heart was still racing, and I was nervous as shit. My newfound fortune was burning a hole in my pocket, and I didn't even have a chance to pocket it yet. I was ready to go cop that fucking Fendi bag I'd seen on display yesterday. One thing a bitch like me didn't do was stunt with a fakey, no fucking way.

Parking my car, I hopped out quickly and checked in, retrieved my room key and went up to my room. When I stepped in the room, I felt safe, and my nerves started to calm just a little. I clicked on the TV to see if the robbery was broadcasting live, but to my surprise, it wasn't. *Maybe later*. I dumped the money out on the bed, throwing myself in it like I had just come up on a million bucks. That's what it felt like because I was dead broke, on my ass. My main dick cut me off because his wife caught us in the act.

"Yessss." I couldn't believe I got away with that shit so easily. *Maybe I should hit another place?* Nah, shit was too sweet to be true and I wasn't gonna press my luck. Momma didn't raise no fool, fuck that.

Derrick

Damn, I swear, fucking Desire today was better than fucking Keisha last night. Maybe it was because my baby momma be on her trip shit. Nigga really tired of all the nagging she did. I had to admit it was something besides my kids that kept a nigga coming back. Something gotta give though, because my bitch was a good girl and didn't deserve what I was doing. For now, though, I didn't want to give this up. A nigga was having his cake and enjoying it too, but I swear Desire sucked that dick like she entered a marathon.

Since I stayed out last night, I decided to stay inside all day with my woman. Part of the reason is because she sucked and fucked all the energy a nigga had. I wasn't tripping though, because I owed it to her to play house. She deserved it. I cut my phone off so I could give her my undivided attention, but not before I sent Keisha a text, asking did I leave my gun by her crib. I didn't notice my shit was gone until I went to take my clothes off. I went straight to my hip, but nothing was there. I had to have left it there, because I remember placing in on her nightstand. Keisha's going to know to lock it in the safe and away from my kids. Even though I lived the life I lived, I didn't need them knowing what the streets said about their pops was true.

Before I turned the phone off, I noticed I had a text from Meeka. I didn't bother reading it, I already know what she wanted. So, I just powered my phone off. I kissed Desire on the forehead, looking down at my lil baby. She wasn't like any of the bitches around here. A nigga could get jammed up today or tomorrow and it's facts she will rock with a nigga when it's time to roll. Right then and there, looking at her while she slept in my arms, I decided I was moving out of this dump. No matter how much she cleaned, cooked and served a nigga like a king, it'll never be the castle she deserved. She must've felt me staring at her, because she began to stir in my arms, coming out of the dick coma I placed her in.

"Baby, how long have I been sleep?" she asked, rubbing the sleep from her eyes.

"Just a couple of hours, love," I replied, getting out the bed to go take a piss.

"Where you going?" she asked, sitting up in the bed quickly. Damn, my baby had a nice ass body, tits were very perky. I def had to put a baby in that.

"Nowhere, just to take a piss. You wanna come?" I asked, fucking with her.

"Only if you let me aim it for you," she said, getting out the bed to follow me. She came in the bathroom behind me, but instead of holding my dick, she brushed her teeth.

"You asking me where I'm going, but where the fuck you think you going?" I asked, eyeing her ass while I released the beast.

"Boy, you know a bitch been having to beg to spend time with you. So, I wouldn't dare miss this for no one." She rinsed her mouth then came and gave a nigga some tongue. "Sometimes I feel like you be ashamed of me or something. As long as we've been together, we barely do anything together. I don't even know any of your friends or anything," she said pouting. I hated when she did that shit, it made a nigga feel like he ain't doing something right.

"Aight, you know what? Get dressed. I got a surprise for you."

"Yesss." She ran to the room pulling out clothes and shit, laying them across the bed. "Bae, turn the shower on so the water will get hot. You know how I feel about cold showers."

I turned it on while she pulled every fucking thing out the closet. Damn, I need to take her places more often, I laughed, shaking my head. By the time I started and finished brushing my teeth, Desire stood there with manicured hands on her hips.

"Are you seriously about to take me somewhere?"

"Yeah, now let's shower, you know your ass take forever to get ready."

An hour later, we were finally heading out the door, looking and smelling like a million bucks.

"Before we leave, I gotta stop by Ms. Ethel and give her this smoke and pick up my keys. I almost forgot my shit. Scrappy ass bet not be joy riding in my shit either, or you gone see a nigga get fucked up today."

"Well, you know every time you get him to wash your cars that's what he does. I can't believe Ms. Ethel really smokes. That woman is like one hundred years old."

"I really think if she didn't, it would kill her. Fuck, it would kill me if I didn't contaminate my lungs. I don't understand why the shit ain't legal yet."

"I seen on the news the other day, if you get caught with just a little on you, the police only write you a ticket or something. If that shit is happening, I know the shit will be legalized any minute."

"Ms. Ethel," I said, approaching her porch.

"Come in," she yelled through the door.

"I got that package for you."

"Boy, what took yo butt so long?" I could have went blind waiting on yo ass. You know this old cataract taking over the ole woman. I been asking Pastor John to pray for me. Ever since he walked into my house and saw me smoking, he ain't been back over here. Shoot, if you ask me, ain't no difference between me getting acquainted with Mary Jane, when half the congregation still hung over from what's the name of that club? ABC?"

"Nah, Ms. Ethel, U.P.T. short for Uptown." Me and Desire fell out laughing.

"Yeah, that's it, U.P.T. and please let's not forget that son of his. That boy Jo Jo is just as confused as my poor baby running around here smoking that crack. Anyway, what took you so long again?" she asked just as I pulled a pound of that good shit from under my shirt. "You know what? You don't even have to answer that. I'm glad you took your time," she smiled big as fuck, while trying to hold her dentures up at the same time. I handed that shit to her and bounced.

"We'll see you later, Ms. Ethel. I'm taking my baby out tonight," I said, grabbing Desire's hand, knowing Ms. Ethel would talk a hole in our heads if we let her.

"It's 'bout time," I heard behind our back.

"What?" I asked, trying to see if I heard her correct.

"See you later."

Damn, even Ms. Ethel's old ass know I don't take Desire out. I gotta get better with taking care of home. Just as we were stepping outside, I saw Scrappy pull up in my whip, blasting Zapp and Roger's "Computer Love."

"Where the fuck you been in my shit, nigga?" I asked, just as he was making his way to the other side opening the door. "Oh, hell no! This ain't no muthafuckin dope rental, nigga. Yo ass had better not have no crumbs in my shit."

"Come on now, baby. You know a nigga ain't wasting nothing, especially crumbs." He smiled, all glassy eyed and shit.

"Give me my muthafuckin keys and nigga, don't nobody listen to that bullshit," I said, snatching my keys. "What? Why you still standing there?"

"Waiting on you to pay me, D."

"You put gas in my shit?"

"Mane, I was waiting on you to pay me, but I got you. I promise I'ma fill your shit back up."

"Nigga please, you said that same shit last time," I said, hopping in my truck.

"Damn, you going to jack a nigga like that?"

"Fucking right, let that car wash be on the house, my nigga," I said, pulling off and turning that bullshit off he had blasting. *Muthafuckin "Computer Love,"* I thought, shaking my head.

Yolanda Moore

D.J.

"Boy, yo daddy gone beat yo muthafuckin ass if he catch you out here and lil nigga, I don't want no part of it."

"Let me worry about my pops, nigga, stop dick riding," I said laughing. I went on to pocket the gun I stole from my mother's nightstand this morning.

"Where you get yo piece from? Let me hold it, boy," Brandon asked me as if that would ever happen.

"Fuck no, you already know nobody touches my dick except my bitch, my gun or my money, homie."

"Nigga, why you capping? I never knew yo young ass had a bitch. You not getting that lil dick wet," Brandon laughed.

"Boy, ya dumb. Bitch, I been getting wet and I ain't talking 'bout a supa soaka."

"Yeah, nigga, you been pissing in the bed," Chris said, while everybody laughed at his wack ass joke.

"Nigga, what the fuck your grown ass doing hanging with us anyway? Ole bitch ass muthafucka, don't nobody fuck with you cuz word in the slums is, you working with the people. So, why you here again?" I asked while my focus was on my phone. I was making a post on the 'Gram. I had taken a picture earlier with the gun showing on my hip. My caption said, "Six bullets left, I wonder where the other ones went."

It was meant to be a statement, not a question. Truth be told, I had never caught a body. But nobody had to know that, especially not my parents. They didn't have a clue I had any social media accounts, or that I even skipped school to hustle in the Southside Projects. They would kill me if they knew I was spending time here, instead of being at school. So far, I hadn't gotten caught up and I didn't have any plans to either.

"Lil nigga, you better respect my mind and respect your elders, before I spank that ass like that nigga Derrick should've been doing."

"Boy, fuck you. There ain't a nigga on Earth that will lay hands on me and live to talk about it," I said, taking my attention away from my phone, pulling my pants up.

"Hold up, wait. Wait, just hold up," Brandon said, stepping between us. That nigga knew none of these niggas put fear in my heart. Especially a bum ass nigga whose bitch ass wouldn't bust a grape in a fruit fight.

"Lil boy, you better thank God for putting this nigga Brandon in yo life, cuz he just saved it." I went for my hip, but was stopped by B. I was ready to show Chris's ass I was thankful for a lot, but definitely not a nigga stopping me from sending his ass to the dirt.

"My nigga, it's not the time nor place. The streets is watching. We can knock that nigga dick in the dirt later but killing the whole projects ain't gone work. You already know you never leave any witnesses," he whispered, so I was the only one that heard the words he spoke. Without saying anything else, I accepted the blunt out of Brandon's hand and took a long ass drag to calm my nerves.

"Let's move the fuck around before I do something I can't take back," I said as I walked off backwards, watching my back until we hopped in the crack rental.

"Nigga, pass me the blunt. I know you mad and shit, but don't take the shit out on the smoke, my nigga." He laughed and so did I, but for reasons other than the situation that had transpired. People always told me how much I not only resembled my father but acted like him as well. I never seen the shit until I got angry. If you ask me, we were the spitting image when a nigga was in his chest.

"You know I would've really wet that boy up, right?" Brandon just looked at me sideways. "Nigga, what?"

"Ain't no nigga what. You gotta keep in mind what we out in these streets for, especially when we going against everything ya pops worked hard for. For one, moving ya spoiled ass out the slums. Everybody ain't able, my nigga. I'm just saying, so don't let none of these lowlife ass niggas fuck it up. A lot of these niggas out here envy you, D.J., so don't forget that shit," Brandon said, turning up the music, not giving me time to respond but to reflect on his words. I did because in all realness, what he said is the truth—like they were words from the Bible.

"I looked down at my vibrating phone, seeing my sister was calling. She must be letting me know she was on the bus on her way home from school.

"What? It's about that time?" Brandon asked, knowing I had to go to the bus stop so I could walk home with my sister as if we went to school together.

"Yeah, bro," I said, acknowledging him, but my mind still wondered to his words earlier. I always took into consideration what my nigga said, knowing he was only pulling my coat tail. I just hated the fact that niggas see me and see my pops, but it ain't even that type of party with me. I'm not trying to eat off his plate. I wanted a nigga to respect my mind because of who I am, not because of my bloodline. I knew exactly how to handle the shit thought. Anytime a muthafucka tried to drop they nuts on me, I'ma make them bitches pick they shit up and tuck 'em straight up. They can either respect it or check it.

"A'ight, my nigga, I'ma fuck with you later. You already missed two days out the school week, so I'ma catch up with you for the weekend."

"A'ight, catch you later, bro," I said as we slapped hands embracing one another.

"And nigga, don't sweat that shit from earlier. We gods, nigga, and muthafuckas like Chris will always be our servants," Brandon was saying as I stepped out the car as the bus was pulling up to drop my sister off.

"Brother, what's good?" my sister asked, giving me a hug like she hadn't seen me in years.

"Nothing, same shit, sis," I said laughing. "Why the fuck you acting like you didn't just see me this morning? Like yo ass really miss me. What you want? You gotta want something," I said as we separated from our embrace.

"What is that?" she asked, looking at my waist frowning.

"What's what?" I asked in return, but I knew exactly what she was talking about.

"Is that a gun?" she asked, with her hand on her hip.

"Mind ya business and let's get home."

"Boy, I know you not gonna bring that in the house. Momma gone shit a brick if she finds that in your room." We started walking towards our house.

"Mane, I'm not worried about Momma. She gives us privacy, so I know she not gone stumble across it unless yo big-head ass rat me out."

"Boy, Daddy don't breed rats, you got me fucked up."

"You know what? Yo ass better watch that dirty mouth of yours before I wash it out with soap," I told her, changing the subject because the conversation at hand was not up to be discussed.

"I wish you'd stop acting like you the oldest, nigga. We are twins and I'm not a baby."

"You're going to always be a baby to me and I'm eleven minutes older than you, punk."

"Whatever. I know you trying to change the subject, but don't get caught up because you know every time you do,

Momma and Daddy take the shit out on me," she said, walking into the crib.

"Yeah, they do take it out on you, until you start crying like a baby," I yelled behind her.

I smelled Momma's cooking as soon as I stepped through the door. *That woman know she can throw down*, I thought smiling as I walked toward the kitchen right on Derrion's heels.

"What the hell are y'all fussing about now?" Momma asked when we walked in and took a seat at the table.

"Nothing," we both said at the same time.

"Alright, y'all don't have to include me in y'all conversation, but I'm still hip to the game," Mom said as she stood over the hot stove.

"Ma, we know you not hip, if you are saying you are," my sister said as we both held our phones in our hands, texting or checking social media.

"I'm not gonna let y'all two determine what I am," Mom said, hitting me with her dish towel and kissing me on the top of my head. "Listen, I've been waiting on the both of you to get home to ask have y'all see your daddy's gun? He texted earlier, asking me if he left it."

"No," I said flatly but Derrion didn't answer. I could feel her burning a hole through me, so I kicked her under the table.

"No, Momma, I didn't. You know how Poppa can be always misplacing things. Did you check your room?" she asked Momma, playing the shit off good. I knew this will cost me, but it's a price I'm willing to pay.

"I did check, but you're right. Derrick is always misplacing his stuff. He knows how I feel about that type of shit in my house anyway," she said as she stood to go retrieve her phone. I wondered if she knew Pops had his stash in the garage or if she was just stunting and putting on a show for us.

Probably was. I know I shouldn't keep my heat in here, but I had to. Fuck, if I didn't protect where we rest our head, my pops sure in the fuck wasn't here to put in work. He was too busy chasing pussy. That is one of the reasons I needed to get my cake up, because I know my dad would cut my mom off and I refused to see her stuck out there.

The Street Will Talk

Jo Jo

Finally, I decided to go home. For two days, I was held up in the room. I was spooked the fuck out from watching the news and looking out the window every time a light shined in my room, from somebody pulling up in the parking lot or leaving out. The first day in the hotel, I had to throw back a Xanax before I drove myself crazy. A bitch was looking like Smokey off *Friday* when his fine ass was in the chicken coop.

All I remember after taking a hot shower was collapsing on top of the hundreds and twenties I couldn't stop counting. Speaking of, I should go back and slap that bitch Judith for playing on a bitch. I told her ass all hundo's and she took it upon herself and added twenties to my stash. A bitch can't complain though. Anyway, all I remember before dozing off was how I was going to spend my newfound fortune.

I must've fallen into a deep sleep because the next time I woke up, the repeat news was broadcasting the robbery I had gotten away with. My mind was racing thinking I'd been caught. *Maybe I had left a fingerprint behind? Maybe the damn cameras were working*, I thought. I was so caught up into what the investigator was reporting I didn't even remove the hundred-dollar bill stuck to my face with slob. When I woke up, I quickly searched for the remote control so I could turn up the volume.

"Today at Checks and Loans, there was an armed robbery committed around lunch time. The culprit walked into this checks and loans positioned behind me, demanding this employee Ms. Judith, to fill the bag with money or else. Judith what would you like to say?" The camera then focused in on the old hag.

"Eh, I just want to say how thankful I am to be alive and I'm grateful the animal who did this to us, decided not to hurt

65

me. After putting a gun to my head, he threatened to kill my cat Peaches. I just... I..." she cried through the camera, not able to complete her sentence. Then these muthafuckas had the nerve to zoom in on the cat that probably wasn't. Quickly switching back to the news investigator, she continued with the segment.

"If you have any information or the known whereabouts of the person that committed this crime, call 1-800-343-STOP. Don't take this lightly, because anyone who would threaten to kill an innocent little cat is capable of anything. Back to you, Sabrina."

I cut the TV off without speaking a word. That was two days ago, and I felt I was in the clear. Still no suspects and honestly, after watching the news, no one could tell that was me on footage. Nobody has ever seen me dressed as a man, even my parents wouldn't know it's me. That was my cue to gather up the money and get the fuck on down. A big smile was plastered across my face, because there were still no suspects and I had really gotten away with the shit.

Even though I had only come up on thirty-five thousand, that wasn't a lot. If my ass would've been caught, it damn sure wouldn't have been worth it. Looking at my current situation, *I was as happy as a punk in a dick factory*, I thought smiling. I needed to figure out how I was going to either make this money last or see what my next hustle would be. I have to bless my mother, not that she needs it, buy another used car, trick off on my snack (my dude) and give Dirty Di a few racks. I would for sure be just as broke as I was a few days ago. Today though, I will conquer and let tomorrow worry about itself.

I dressed, grabbed my keys and headed over to my mom's, hoping my dad wasn't there. Sometimes the nigga forgot he came from the same struggle as the rest of us, and I would hate to bump heads with his holier than thou ass. Did he not know we were all born into sin? Now I'm heading out to Ponchatoula, to Cypress Estates, where my family now resides. I had about a forty-five-minute drive ahead of me. My mom and dad stayed on Cypress Drive in a gated community. I must admit, the spot is peaceful and every corner you turned, you didn't have to worry about drug addicts, untamed kids, hustlers and killers.

"With so much drama in the LBC, it's kinda hard being Snoop D-O Double G but I, somehow some way keep coming up with funky ass shit like every single day."

I rolled up to the guard shack in Cypress Estates like I owned a house in that muthafucka bumping "Gin and Juice," by Snoop Doggy Dogg. Rolling the window down, the white security guard frowned as that loud escaped the window. I turned the music down to hear what his white ass was saying, because I was dumbfounded like a special ed.

"Welcome to Cypress Estates, identification please." He stood his sexy pink ass there holding a clipboard, with them tight ass shorts, showing a bitch his dick print. I grabbed my purse, handing him my ID, he looked over the damn clipboard a few times before he handed me my shit back.

"Sorry, your name isn't on the guest list," he said, looking as if he was sincere.

"What?" I asked with a stupid look of not understanding written across my face.

"Sir—"

"Oh, fuck no! I know you didn't just disrespect a bitch like that!" I said, acting a damn fool removing my silver hoops.

"Could you calm down, ma'am, the hostility isn't called for."

"Oh, yes the fuck it is, calling me sir. But I know one muthafuckin thing." I reached in the back seat, grabbing my

Nike's to strap up on his ass. If I was in the hood, there was no such thing as getting ready to bust ass. Where I'm from, you better be ready. "You need to tap on them computer keys and place my name in like you woulda done if I was your kind. Don't fucking play with me," I said, getting out not bothering closing the door. I didn't give a fuck about the line of cars piled behind me either.

"Ma'am, just give me a second. Can I see your identification once more?" he asked me, turning beet red while backing up into the guard shack.

"Yes, you can," I said, extending it back to him. I leaned inside the shack's door as he typed, watching the computer screen as well. As sure as shit stink, my name didn't come up, it said "invalid." Now was my turn to turn pink if there were such a thing.

"Go the fuck around." I waved my hands, embarrassed like a muthafucka.

"You have to leave, or I will have to contact the proper authorities."

"Fuck the proper authorities! Give me a damn minute to call my parents to see what the fuck the problem is!" I said, madder than a bitch right now. I had no fucking understanding. This had to be a mistake, I'm too divafied for this.

"Hello?" I heard my mom say through the gotdamn phone.

"Why in the hell am I not able to get past the guard shack?" I yelled.

"I don't know, sweetheart, but put Billy on the phone." I pressed speaker because I wasn't letting his ass touch my shit. "Ma, go 'head," I said, trying to calm the hell down. I know it had to be my father that done some bull crap like this.

"Yes, I'm sorry. Billy, this must be a mistake you can let her through."

"Ma'am, I can't do that without her being on the visiting list. So, if you don't mind coming to fill out the proper paperwork, I can let her in."

"Damn," I said, jerking my phone away from his mouth. "Do you have any other words in your vocabulary besides proper? I have more than that and my black ass didn't attend an Ivy League college." I rolled my eyes. "Ma, just come do the paperwork before you have to call in a favor from God on my behalf." I hung up, not giving her time to say anything else.

I got back in my car and pulled to the side to wait for my dear mother as I smoked the rest of my weed. Thank God for this, because in any minute I was about to commit one of the Ten Commandments. Thou shalt not kill.

Yolanda Moore

Derrick

It's been a few days since Desire had a nigga held hostage with that sweet pussy she was blessed with. I don't know what has gotten into my baby, but it's like she been taking lessons and I been enjoying every moment of it. If a nigga wasn't sure about anything else, I know we had to have made a baby or two. For now, I had other things to deal with that were more important than getting my dick wet. Like dealing with this bitch nigga Chris. Besides, it felt like a nigga been fucking every day for a month straight. I pulled my phone out to hit my nigga Lunchmeat up.

"What the fuck you doing, nigga?" I asked as soon as the phone connected.

"Chilling," he said, grunting in the phone.

"Nigga, it don't sound like you chillin," I laughed.

"Damn, can a nigga get they dick sucked in peace?"

"What? Do yo ditty, nigga, but be finished by the time I roll up. We got shit to do."

"Aight, where we meeting at? You know I don't let nobody know where I rest my head, not even my moms, nigga."

"The usual, my nigga. I know it's been a while since we put in that work, but everything's the same. I'll see you in a few." I hung up. I had quickly switched to beast mode, especially now that it's time to put in that work.

I got dressed after I showered and grabbed my nine before I headed out the door. When I made it to the trap, I headed straight to the basement. Besides Lunch and I, some new nigga I didn't know was there too. I didn't like shit around the niggas I know, so you know how I felt about a muthafucka I didn't know. I made a mental note to make sure to check my nigga on that shit.

"This my nigga, Kane. Kane, this D," Lunch said, reading my mind.

I just looked at the nigga Kane because there was definitely no need for an introduction.

"So, what's poppin? Who we hitting?" I didn't want to ask too many questions on the phone.

"Chris."

"Word? Say less," he said, knowing what time it is.

"You got something to say?" I asked the nigga Kane as he just looked. "Any questions?"

"No questions, my nigga. The boss man gave the word and I know when you speak, to take the shit like a command from God."

I just looked at this clown ass muthafucka.

"I heard that boy be by them fuck boys on the lake because he couldn't afford a plate at our table. The last day I seen that boy in the projects was the day he got into it with D.J."

When the dude said my son's name, you woulda thought I was possessed, the way my neck turned damn near backwards to face him.

"Lunch, who the fuck is this nigga again?" I said, pulling my gun.

"Wait, God." Kane held his hands up as if he could stop a bullet from piercing his skull.

"What the fuck you mean, got into it with D.J.? When the fuck was he over here?" I asked, feeling some type of way. This is the exact reason I moved my fucking kids away from this bitch. One thing I know about being knee deep in the streets, the first move a nigga make is to target your family to get at you. Niggas in the streets knew there wasn't shit they could possibly do to me that would affect me, but touching my family was a whole different story.

"I just saw they were passing words, but Jr. handled his business. I swear the nigga would've been tasting the dirt if he would have made one false move, but lucky for him D.J. bounced, my nigga, I swear," he said as my gun rested under the nigga chin.

"Just like a debt can be inherited with death, so can beef. There ain't a nigga on earth that I will allow to touch my family and live to tell about it." That nigga didn't know it, but he was living on borrowed time. *This shit with him had just became personal*, I thought, pulling my ski mask over my face. It's show time and not at the Apollo. I would definitely be painting the town red.

Yolanda Moore

Lakeside Boys (Inside the Trap House)

"Mane, pass the fucking weed, nigga. That is why I don't be wanting yo ass to put in, nigga," one of the Lakeside Boys told Chris while playing the new Xbox.

"Nigga, miss me with them pill head games. As long as I put my money up and you put yours, I'ma puff this muthafucka however long I want to, nigga," Chris said, hittin the blunt again before passing it. "Now you can have this bullshit. I don't even know where you get this garbage from. Next time I'm in charge of finding the smoke," he said as the dude accepted the weed.

"Yeah, you talking all that shit, but you always wrap them big ugly dry ass lips around my shit," he laughed, but his smile was quickly removed once he heard the door being kicked in like the SWAT team was coming for them. Without being told, they both threw their hands up, instead of going for the gun that sat between them on the couch.

"Everybody, get the fuck down or lay the fuck down!" the nigga Kane shouted like he was in charge. I had to look at this nigga like, *the fuck*? Who he thought he was? Biggs off *Shottas*? Yeah, I definitely had to check the situation but for now, I had other agendas to tend to.

"The fuck! Bitch ass nigga, you heard the man, on the fucking ground!" I shouted, smacking dude upside his head with my gun, knocking the blunt out his mouth.

"Damn, mane, you ain't have to do that shit," Chris had the nerve to say as the other nigga got with the program.

"Shut the fuck up, you itch. I do what the fuck I want." I hit Chris' ass too, knocking him back down to his size. When he dropped to the floor, I bent down, snatching his head up by his dreads. "Do you or I have the muthafuckin gun? I thought so." I slammed his head down into the wooden floor, busting his mouth open, hoping I broke some of the nigga's teeth.

"Spread out, I'ma stay here with them. How many more people they got in this bitch?" I asked the other nigga. I know Chris was too busy crying about that lil scratch. *Bitch nigga*, I thought.

"No one," he quickly answered.

"Nigga, on life, you better be speaking the truth. Go search the house and if you see a muthafuckin roach moving, I want that bitch stepped on." Before the words could get out my mouth, they both took off in opposite directions.

"Where's the money and the drugs, Chris?" I looked down at him while my gun stayed trained on his head. I wanted this nigga to know this wasn't a joke, and I didn't come to play any games, period.

"We ain't got shit, mane." I took my gun and hit the next nigga in the head, since Chris was already in bad shape.

"What about you, home boy? Where the muthafuckin shit at? Y'all niggas can lose ya life over another nigga's shit if you want." I cocked the Glock. "Aight, you niggas think I'm playing?"

"Damn, tell this nigga where the shit at, I'm not trying to die behind this bullshit. Them niggas ain't paying us enough for this, fuck that!" Chris yelled to the other nigga on beside of him while teeth and blood gushed out his mouth.

"Good boy," I said, patting Chris' bitch ass on the head like a dog. "Oh, Chris, this for fucking with my kid."

"D, mane, hold up…"

Boom

I cut that nigga off before he had time to plead his case. Whatever he had to say, I was deaf to the bullshit.

"Fuck boy. Aight, now to you. Ace, you gonna take Chris' advice and tell me where the Lake Boys keep their shit? I hope I don't have to fuck you up either, do I?"

"No, mane," this nigga said, crying like a bitch.

"Damn, bro, everything alright out here?" Lunchmeat and Kane ran from the back tryna see if everything was still under control.

"I'm good, but I told y'all niggas I didn't come here to talk. A nigga would be on a talk show if that's what I wanted to do."

"Everything clear, but we got like ten minutes to clear this bitch," Lunchmeat said.

"Let's go, nigga." I pushed dude with the gun. As soon as we made it to the safe, dude opened the safe with no problem.

"Our Father, who art in heaven, hallowed be thy name..."

Boom

The dude didn't even have time to finish The Lord's Prayer, before he met his faith, whatever that may be.

"I don't give a fuck what you niggas take. You know I only came here to get at Chris," I told them. I never fucked with blood money, if I bust a nigga grape it was for disrespecting me. As for my paper, I hustled for what I wanted. There was too much money out here to be made and taking from the next man just wasn't in my blood.

"Time's up, bro," Lunch yelled and we headed for the front door the same way we came in this bitch. Lunchmeat first, Kane, then me.

Boom

Boom

"What the fuck?" Lunch shouted when he turned around. Kane was laid out breathless. "Damn, that's my first cousin, nigga."

"Nigga, you shoulda told me that, my bad," I told him, not knowing if his crazy ass was gone pop off.

Instead, he shrugged it off, placing his chin in between his index and thumb as if he was in deep thought.

"What the fuck I'ma tell my T-lady? You know what? Fuck it, the nigga owed me and her money. I guess with the insurance policy, we will both get paid now, plus some."

We hopped in the getaway car with three duffle bags full of dog food (heroin), coke and money.

"Nigga, how much he owed you?" I asked Lunchmeat. I just had to know.

"Just twenty dollars," he said, pulling out a lighter and blunt.

"Nigga, you play too much," I laughed. "When did you have time to roll that?" I asked, never seeing when he had the time.

"I didn't, I took it from them niggas back there," he said, dismissing the fact we just left his cousin lifeless back there.

D.J.

"What's the dealie, D?" Brandon asked once I got in the whip.

"You got it, mane," I replied as we slapped hands.

"You been going to school, nigga?"

"Are you seriously asking me about school on a damn Saturday? Leave that school shit up for Monday through Friday," I said as we pulled off from the crib.

"You know if I'm asking it is for a reason," he said with a serious tone.

"Yeah, I went all this week. You know anytime I skip school, I'm always with you, why? What's up?" I asked, waiting to see what his response would be. He never asked me about school, and I was trying to see why today.

"Well, it's apparent you hadn't heard what the streets are saying, and I forgot with you being out here, it's kinda hard to do that."

"Nigga, could you just get to the damn important part of this conversation, instead of beating around the bush?" I told Brandon, becoming real impatient.

"Chris is dead and some of the homies think it's you who is behind the trigger but—" I cut Brandon off, I was bent over laughing.

"Me?" I laughed even harder before I could get my words out. "Niggas really think I killed Chris? That's the funniest shit I heard in a long time." I continued to laugh, trying to catch my breath.

"Yo dogg, that's the same thing I said reaction and all, but I guess by you and Chris passing words, everybody with eyes that can see noticed how heated the argument became. So yeah, the police been coming around questioning niggas about the shit. If you ask me, ya pop's name is written all over this shit. Anybody with a damn brain knows if you cross one of

79

Derrick's people, especially his children, shit could turn sour real fucking quick. That boy TTG (trained to go) all day."

I heard the shit Brandon was saying, but if what the streets were saying was true, I'm in hell and hot water whenever my pops caught up with me. All of a sudden, his banger on my hip had become very heavy and I had started to regret ever touching my father's shit.

"Mane, they say there was three bodies left on the crime scene. All them niggas' heads were blown off execution style, so you know them niggas meant business." I listened as B kept talking, but then my mind wandered.

"Where did this shit happen?" I asked.

"Lakeside," Brandon looked at me with a serious look on his face as we sat at the red light, waiting for it to turn green.

"Damn," was all I could say.

I went to school with some niggas from Lakeside and even though I hadn't pulled the trigger, and niggas knew it was my pops, I had trouble surely coming my way. *Fuck what you heard*, I thought. Yeah, I might have not grown up in the Southside Projects, but that dump shit ran through me when it came to a nigga disrespecting my mind. I was always as cool as a cucumber, but I knew soon I would have to teach niggas a lesson. Class was definitely in session. Trust me when I say the apple didn't fall too far from the true. *Like father, like son*, was the last thought that ran through my mind before the light turned green.

***

Finally making it to the projects, there wasn't a soul in sight. Ever since I was knee-high to a duck, this bitch stayed booming, but with all the shit Brandon just ran down to me, the projects looked like a ghost town. I knew even when Ms.

Ethel was in the house and wasn't on her porch, sitting in her rocking chair, the people (police) had definitely come through.

"Damn, shit really serious, huh?" I asked Brandon as we got out the car.

"Nigga, I told you! Fuck you thought, I was playing? Just as we closed the door a car with tinted windows rolled by slowly, the back window came down and the car came to a complete stop. I didn't have to grow up in the projects or watch a fucking gangsta movie to know when trouble was coming my way. My hand went straight to my hip and so did Brandon's.

"You don't have to do all that, blood clot," I heard a Jamaica voice shout from the window. That boy was definitely Lakeside all day long.

"Fuck," I said under my breath where I was sure no one heard it.

"What the fuck you want, clot?" Brandon said as he pulled his gun off his hip completely and I followed suit. I wasn't letting my boy draw by himself. Fuck that!

"Mi casa es su casa," he said, stepping out the car. "Isn't that what you bread-crumb-snatching nigglets thought when you came snatching everything that belonged to me, huh?" As soon as dude stepped up to me with the gun to my head. I could hear Ms. Ethel step out on her porch.

"I called the police and I'm recording this as we speak. So, I suggest y'all get y'all asses away from here, and leave them young men alone." In the distance I could hear the police sirens and knew I would live to see another day.

"Let ya father know Glo looking for him and I want his head," dude said, taking his thumb across his throat as if he was sliding a head off the shoulders.

As soon as Glo and the other two niggas with assault rifles hopped back into the tinted window car, Brandon and I ran. Not because we almost died, but the sirens were louder and that was an indication they were closer to the area. One thing we weren't was stupid. We made it to the back of the projects just in time to put the guns up.

"My nigga, you know when ya pops hear about this shit, he gone turn B.R. upside down, right?"

I just shook my head because I knew shit had really just got real, if there was such a thing.

***

By the time Monday morning rolled around, it was time to face the shit at my school. I made it through first and second period like a breeze, but at lunch time I didn't know if I would be able to say the same. As usual, I went by Derrion's English class to pick her up. We always chilled together for lunch time.

"What's up, bro?" she asked, kissing me one my cheek and looping her arm in mine.

"Nothing, how was your English class?" I asked like I always did.

"The same ole shit. I really can't wait until we graduate. I'm so tired of high school, I'm ready for college. I heard it's a lot of partying."

"Yeah, everything isn't what muthafuckas say it is, and where did you hear that from? That is the stupidest shit I heard. If you ask, me, that is the time you should be putting all the partying outfits up, and start bringing out the two-piece Gucci suits," I said, knowing she would love that. As long as she could play dress-up, my sister was game for anything.

"Now that's something I can't wait for." She smiled at the thought when we entered the cafeteria.

Just like always, the place was packed, even though no one actually ate the food. It was just the spot to be. Where you can be yourself, show your talents (singing, rapping or dancing), holla at the girls whether they were available or not and let me not forget, make out with your girl.

"There's Beyonca," Derrion said as if I didn't see my baby coming my way.

Even though they couldn't stand one another, I was happy to see her beautiful smiling face, because I had missed it all weekend long. My girl and my sister used to be the best of friends growing up. Unfortunately, I was the common denominator that separated them from the love they once held for each other. Hey, what can I say? Shit happens. My sister didn't like the fact I decided to go out with not only her friend, but her best friend, at the gate. My girl felt I showered my sister with two men.

If you ask me, they're both always acting like it's that time of the month. So, I tried to spend my time equally between the both of them. Some people thought it to be weird that me and my sister were so close, but I didn't. Fuck, Derrion has been here with me since day one and I refuse to let anyone come between me and my blood.

"You know I saw her all up in them Lakeside Boys' faces the week you skipped school, right?" Derrion said and I instantly felt some type of way.

Neither my girl nor my sister knew the beef that is going on. So even though I'm not going to speak on it now, I definitely had plans on checking Beyonca on the little situation. If there was any truth in what Derrion said, and she has never lied to me before, then we definitely have a problem. For now, I plan to keep the peace. So as soon as we walked up on each other, I wrapped my arms around her, pulling her close to me so I could taste her lips.

"Get a damn room," my sister said, stomping off to go meet up with her clique of bougie friends.

"So, what is this I'm hearing about you being with them Lakeside niggas?" I said, checking her temp.

"No, baby, why would you ask me some shit like that? You know I don't get down with the Lakeside. I'ma straight Southside baby, and you know I rep your set everywhere I go. Besides, I know not to play with you." She kissed my lips as she stayed tucked inside my arms.

One thing I know about my sister is she would never do anything to hurt me. So, somebody is lying to me and I had a feeling I would be finding out soon.

Derrick

I had finally made good on my promise and moved my girl out of the Southside Projects. Even though we left our domain, I will always be a Southside baby until the death of me. So, letting the place go was out of the question. It will only become my home away from home and be kept to put to good use. Today, I decided to show my face in the hood, so I could put my ear to the streets and see what they had to say.

"Yo, my nigga, what's the business?" Lunchmeat asked as I stepped outside of my whip.

"Shit, I'm chilling. Lunch, what's for supper, my nigga?"

"Mane, you know what it is everyday life shit, ya heard me? Niggas tryna survive and feed they fam, man," Lunchmeat said, not wanting to say too much because we had company.

"What it do, Killa Kay?" I said, giving that nigga pound. I must admit, dude was solid, but I wouldn't dare let another nigga in my business to take the stand. And if Lunch would have spoken our business in front of anybody but God, he would definitely be meeting his cousin.

"Fuck, I'm tryna see now, that's why a nigga out here tryna eat now. You know I'm grindin everyday all day. TTG all day, boy."

"Ain't a muthafuckin thing ever been wrong with that. If it ain't 'bout the hustle, nothing else matters," I said.

"Shit, tell that to these lil niggas out here on that rah-rah shit. Nigga got bumped to the earth the other day on Lakeside, but niggas don't know who it was that did it. Rumor is them Lakeside Boys coming for our top. I just hope they asked the Lord for forgiveness already, because I shoot first and ask questions later. Fuck giving them niggas time to repent. They should've thought of that shit before they crossed that muthafuckin threshold. My lil brother Brandon said them niggas pulled guns on them the other day."

"Brandon? Ain't that the lil nigga that be with my son?"

"Yeah," Lunch answered before Killa Kay could open his mouth.

"Yeah, that's my lil bro and I'm feeling some type of way. Them niggas straight got me fucked. Whoever the other nigga beside Chris and Kane was next of kin to that nigga, Glo. Word is all dude's head was blown off. His own momma couldn't identify him. The nigga Glo sent word he didn't give a fuck about the drugs or money, but the only satisfaction for him would be to behead the niggas responsible. Fuck what them niggas heard 'bout the Southside Projects. It's jackin season and I ain't talking 'bout money. I'm straight jacking a nigga when it comes to me and mine. Straight like that."

My ears perked up when Killa Kay said Brandon was his brother and that Glo had whipped down on him. I knew for facts my son had to be with him. Them two lil niggas was like peanut butter and jelly. I needed to get word to D.J. to stay his hardheaded ass away from the projects. I also made a mental note to check his ass about my gun his mom swears I didn't leave at the crib. I knew it's not a coincidence he was seen the same day flashing a fucking gun. Matter of fact, let me call this lil nigga now. I called his phone immediately and on the third ring, there was a connection.

"Poppa! Come to the school now!" I heard my baby girl Derrion yell through the phone before the line disconnected.

"Nigga, let's go," I quickly said to Lunch. "Something going on at the school." My heart raced at what seemed to be a mile a minute. Killa hopped in the back seat without question. Something in my heart told me some shit just wasn't right.

86

Finally pulling up to the school, I was able to park in the fire zone for quicker access. Just as we were hopping out the car, Glo and his boys were pulling up too.

"What the fuck these niggas doing here?" Killa asked and I could hear his gun being pulled back to place one in the chamber.

"Be easy, my nigga. Too many pigs (police) running around here and on top of that, too many witnesses," I said to both of them cuz I already knew how my niggas got down.

"No doubt, but I swear if these wannabe Rastas come for my top, I ain't gone have no problem pushing they top back, straight like that," Killa said, ready to show and prove why he was given the name in the first place.

"I heard you boys was ready to pon de river," Glo said as him and his crew approached us.

"What the fuck you clowns want?" I said, looking at the nigga upside his head. "The only language we speak is knocking a nigga's head off. So, since you blood clots ain't making no noise, I suggest you get the fuck on before I say fuck the police." I stepped closer, mugging these fools, ready to pounce on that nigga.

"Hey, are any of you the parents of Derrick Jones or Maddox Kingston?" a sexy female police officer asked just as shit was about to pop off.

"I'm Derrick's father," I said, not taking my eyes off of Glo's, letting that nigga know right game, wrong muthafuckin nigga.

"So, I'm going to assume you are kin to Maddox," she said, looking at Glo with a notepad in her hand.

"What happened?" I asked, concerned about my son. *Fuck what this nigga talking 'bout, it's apparent he ain't saying much*, I thought.

"Well, there was a fight in the cafeteria," the sexy female officer divulged.

"What the fuck do you mean?" Glo asked and I could tell he was heated, but I wasn't worried at all, because D.J. been in the ring since he came out the womb. My son was an army by himself.

"Mr. Kingston, just calm down. They were both assessed, and they are both ok. Young Mr. Kingston only had a few bumps and bruises, but nothing little boys aren't used to. I think you both need to have a talk with the school and if you both don't mind, we'd like to speak with you both downtown."

"What the fuck you mean?" we all asked at the same time. Niggas hated talking to the cops unless they had something to say, and it was big facts Lakeside and Southside kept the beef in the streets.

"Is this mandatory?" said Derrick.

"Yes, it is. If we are going to have any problems, let us know now and we will handle the situation accordingly," I heard and saw someone walking towards us out the corner of my eye, another cop.

"What does this have to do with two children having a lil ass tussle at school?" Killa Kay spoke up before I could.

"Who are you again?" the female officer asked, notepad still in hand. Killa Kay threw his hands up.

"Just a friend of the family. My nigga, let me know what you need me to do."

"Call Desire and tell her to come pick up the twins for me, because it's going to be hard for Keisha to get off from work. And let Desire know to have bond money on standby just in case." I tossed them my keys and both Glo and I was escorted to the back of the cop car. A muthafuckin place a nigga had no plans on ever visiting ever again in life, even if I wasn't under arrest. *Fuck!*

***

After hours of being questioned about the murders from the other night, a nigga was tired. I came out of that muthafucka prepared to walk. My phone was dead, and I didn't want to use the phone or wait for a ride. I was ready to get the fuck away as far as I could, before them muthafuckas dug something out their ass to pin on a nigga and decide to lock me up.

As soon as the door closed behind me, I spotted Desire sitting in the parking lot waiting on a nigga. This shit made me smile big as fuck. I had never been that happy to see her in my life. As soon as she spotted me, she hopped out to come and meet me halfway.

"What's good, baby girl?" I asked, pulling her close to kiss her lips. Just the few hours I had been in the same building with them muthafuckas, had a nigga missing home as if I had got sent up the road.

"I been out here waiting for you, daddy," she said, smiling up at me.

"Thanks for coming."

"You don't have to do all that. Being here for you is my job and if I had to wait all night, that is exactly what I would have done," she said as we came out of our embrace.

"That's my fucking girl." I smiled. "Now let's get the fuck from around here before I end up giving them bitches something to really question me about," I said, smacking her ass.

Buying my baby a house was the best thing I could have ever done. Since doing so, her spoiled ass hadn't been acting like a brat. A nigga couldn't wait to get home to take away some of this stress I have been through today.

Desire

When I received a call from Killa Kay, I knew immediately something had gone wrong. For one, Derrick has never allowed me or his friends to communicate. So, the first place my mind went to is Derrick was either dead or in jail and if either was the case, neither was good news. When Killa Kay told me to make my way down to the police station with bond money, I was able to breathe a little better.

After picking the twins up from school, I dropped them off at the new house, grabbed a duffle bag full of money and went to pick my man up. Just as I was falling asleep, I saw my nigga being freed. I hurried out the car, running towards him like he had just did a bid in prison, and it was his first day home. That is exactly what it felt like and as soon as we got in my car, I got the fuck as far as I could away from the ops.

On our drive home, Derrick could not keep his hands off me and no lie, he had my pussy soaking wet. As I drove, he slipped his hand under my dress.

"Oh, you don't have nothing on under this fucking dress? What? You was giving my pussy to the next nigga?" he asked me seriously as if I would really do some shit like that.

"Really? Don't fuck with me, Derrick, you know this pussy is yours," I said just as serious, hoping his ass didn't piss me off with that crazy ass bullshit.

"Who you talking to like that?" he asked, leaning over as he rotated my clitoris in a circular motion.

"Nobody," I said, switching my right foot off the gas pedal to my left. I opened my legs as wide as I could for him to gain easy access.

"That's what the fuck I thought. And when I question you 'bout this good wet pussy, don't forget this shit belongs to me."

"Nigga, you gotta show me it's for you. Yo mouth can say anything," I said as I could feel my clit rock up.

"You still talking back?"

"Make me shut up if you have a problem," I said, looking down at him, while also trying to keep my eyes on the road. But right now, it was hard for a bitch to multi-task. "Fuck," I yelled as his thick ass tongue flicked across my clit.

He licked my shit good-good, making me press down on the gas. Thank God I had hit the freeway because I was not trying to crash and burn. I could see the news headlines now, "Thirty-six-year-old woman and boyfriend exchanging sexual favors before smashing into a tree or running a red light."

"Don't run now, talk your shit like you was a minute ago," he said as my left leg held him in a chokehold. This nigga needs to be dragged down to the police station more often. He has never sucked on my pussy this good and right now, his head game was better than great. Tony the Tiger ain't have shit on my baby.

"Fuck, Derrick, suck that shit," I yelled, while closing my eyes for a second. Not for too long, just long enough for my eyes to roll to the back of my head and focus back into place. I could feel an orgasm coming, so I quickly placed my car in cruise mode and enjoyed the ride, grinding my soaking wet juice box on his face.

"Derrick, baby, I'm 'bout to… I'm cumming," I yelled like a crazy woman. I came harder than a muthafucka and was left with a pool on my leather seats. I could feel my juices sliding down the slit of my ass and that only intensified my sexual drive.

Derrick finally came up for air with cum dripping off his bottom lip. I bent over, meeting him face-to-face, licking every drop of me off his mouth. *Damn, I taste good*, I thought as I quickly pressed the gas to make it home.

***

Not even fifteen minutes later, we were pulling in the driveway to finish what we had started.

"Damn it!" I thought aloud, looking ahead at the door it was cracked open.

"What?" Derrick asked, then he realized what caught my attention.

"Wait in the car and don't get out," he said, touching his hip but then figured out he didn't have his gun.

"Wait...baby?" I said, just as he stepped out the car, closing the door in my face. I hopped out right behind him. "Derrick," I called out as he bent down in the flowerpot to retrieve his gun. From that point, it seemed everything began to move in slow motion. "Derrick, noooo!" I screamed just as Derrion opened the door and a hail of bullets ripped through her small body. For a minute, we all stood there frozen in time. I looked up and saw D.J. standing right behind where Derrion now lay as stiff as a board.

"No, no, no, noooooooo. Not my baby girl!" Derrick shouted as he hit his knees and crawled over to Derrion. I could see his soul leaving his body and all principles and values were gone. There was no turning back for him.

"Agggggh! No, no, no somebody call 911. Please don't let my baby die. Not now, God!" If I had to compare Derrick's cry to anything on this planet, it would be like a wounded animal in the wild.

I quickly ran back to my car to grab my purse to retrieve my phone. As I searched for the device I fumbled, going through my purse trembling like a leaf on a tree during hurricane season. Grabbing my phone finally, I dialed the number we were forbidden to dial growing up.

"D.J.," I called out, snapping him out of his comatose mindset. That is when I realized in his left hand, he held a 9mm gun. *What the hell was he doing with a gun?* I know Derrick told me he didn't hold guns in my damn house. He knows how I feel about guns. The one he did talk me into keeping in the house for protection, we kept in a locked box, and I didn't even have the code to it. *So, how did D.J. get the gun?*

"This is 911, what is your emergency?" The call finally connected. Maybe it was just me, but it seemed like fifteen minutes passed as if 911 wasn't the emergency line.

"Yes, there has been an accident at…" I called out my home address.

"Ma'am, just tell me what happened. Stay calm and stay on the line."

"Listen, bitch, could you send a first fucking responder here? I don't have fucking time to answer these stupid ass questions," I said, yelling through the phone right before I hung up. I looked back up at D.J., still stuck in the same place holding the gun, when I realized I had never told him what I needed him to do. I walked up to him, grabbing the gun out of his hands with my shirt.

"Baby, I need you to listen to me, ok? Right now, I need you to be strong, so pull yourself together. We all need to be here for your sister right now, ok? Go to the bathroom and grab me some towels from out the cabinet," I instructed D.J. as I looked him in the eyes, holding him by his shoulders. We had no time to waste. When I finally got D.J. to move out of the spot he had been stuck in since everything unfolded, I turned to Derrick, bending down alongside him.

"Baby, it's not your fault, it is going to be ok. She is going to be ok. Do you understand me?" I asked as I coached him to remain calm. "You didn't mean to shoot her, honey—" He cut me off.

"I didn't do it," he said as snot and tears poured down his face into a mixture.

"What?" I asked, thinking he had lost his mind or his memory.

"I never pulled the trigger."

Just then, D.J. came back to the door holding the towels in his hand. That is when it hit me and made more sense. *D.J. shot Derrion. Poor baby.*

"I'm sorry, it was a mistake. All I saw was Pops holding a gun. My mind fell into protection mode. It was a mistake." D.J. finally spoke and I swear, he sounded like a little six-year-old boy.

"Desire, baby, give him the keys to the car and let him go before the police get here. I can't and won't lose both of them."

"Pops, I can't leave her. I need to stay here."

"Listen to me, son, you have to. If you haven't listened anything I have ever told you in life, I'm begging you, now is the time to obey me." I could hear the sirens in the distance, which meant the cops would be pulling up sooner than later. One thing I know about Derrick is when he spoke, he meant business. So, without further thought, I grabbed D.J. by the hand and escorted him to my car, placing the keys in his hand. I kissed his forehead to encourage him that everything will be just fine. D.J. eventually got with the program and pulled off.

Quickly thinking, I took one of the towels D.J. brought out of the house and wiped his fingerprints off the gun. Just when I was taking the gun from Derrick's hand, his truck was pulling up with Killa Kay inside and Lunchmeat pulling up right behind him. They both hopped out of their trucks, running towards us. The cops hadn't made it yet, but in the distance, I could still hear their alarm sounding.

"Come on, my nigga, we gonna take her to the hospital. We can't just leave her out here bleeding out. Fuck the police. We never depended on them to look out for us and we ain't starting now, my nigga, we all we got."

With that said, Derrick picked Derrion up, pulling her close to his chest. This was the saddest thing I had ever seen in my life, including watching my mom on her deathbed. Derrion's head just hung to the side as if she had no more life inside of her, but I refused to believe this child, my stepchild, would lose her life today.

Once we were all inside the truck, we pulled off just as the first responders were pulling up.

Derrick

Derrion had been in surgery for about two hours when I realized I had not even contacted Keisha. *Fuck!* I know she gonna be madder than a muthafucka, and the longer I waited, the worse the shit would be.

"I have to go make a phone call, I'll be back," I said, squeezing Desire's leg.

"Ok, baby, go handle your business," she responded.

I made a mental note to show her my appreciation. Through all of this, she has had my back and really impressed me the way she had pulled through under pressure. Stepping outside of the hospital to the smoking section, I spotted Lunchmeat. I walked over to him as he leaned over onto the railing, smoking a blunt.

"Nigga, you want to hit this shit?" he asked once I stood beside him, leaning on the rail also.

"Yeah, I actually do, but let me make this phone call to Keisha first. I know after I tell her this shit, she's going to blow the fuck up like the Twin Towers."

After making the call to Keisha, I took Lunch up on his offer and hit the blunt, welcoming the cloud of smoke to contaminate my lungs. I needed this escape and even though the weed is not equivalent to my problems, I still pretended it would take some of the weight off my shoulders.

"I'm sorry this had to happen to you, my nigga. I could only imagine the pain you are going through, but I promise whoever the niggas are responsible, I'm ready to ride on whoever you point the finger at. Just place them niggas in a line-up and I'm giving you my word, them niggas gone be pushing flowers by the end of the week," Lunch said emotionally.

"My nigga, that won't be necessary."

"With all due respect, fuck what you saying, my nigga. I know you not thinking right now, but I'm telling you the move I'm making. You ain't gotta do shit but be here for your baby girl. I'ma do what I do best, straight dumping on niggas and that's on my momma's grave," he said, cutting me off.

"Dog, it was me, it was a mistake, but I'm the reason she up there fighting for her life," I said, realizing at that moment what I needed to do to protect my son. Before Lunch could respond, I heard my name being called.

"Yo! D, bruh, you needed in family waiting room, Keisha made it," my cousin Latray said, taking off back through the entrance of the sliding glass doors. Lunch and I quickly headed that way.

"I need to see my muthafuckin baby!" I heard as soon as I walked through the doors. Keisha was crying hard, and I couldn't lie and say the shit wasn't pulling at a nigga's heartstrings. As soon as she spotted me, she ran towards me, wrapping her arms around me crying her heart out. "Deerrrrrick. I can't lose her, I can't."

"We not gone lose her, Keisha. I promise you we not," I assured her, *or was it more for myself*, I thought as I looked over at Desire, appreciating her understanding throughout this whole ordeal. I placed my attention back on Keisha, trying my best for her to stay calm, but the more I told her everything will be ok, the more she started to hyperventilate. Soon after her not being able to catch her breath, she started seizing right in the middle of the lobby in my arms.

"Help! Somebody, help!" I yelled trying to get someone's attention. Good thing a doctor was just getting off the elevator right in front of where everything was unfolding.

I stepped back from where everything was happening, giving the doctor and nurses room to handle their business. As soon as I did, the same officers who questioned me about the murders committed on Lakeside was standing by my side with a smirk on their face.

Yolanda Moore

Desire

What the fuck was going on? First Derrick getting picked up and questioned about three homicides happening on Lakeside, then D.J. shooting Derrion. Derrick's baby momma Keisha collapsing in the middle of the hospital lobby and now, this muthafuckin shit.

"Desire, call my fuckin lawyer and have him down at the police station ASAP!" Derrick yelled as the police escorted him in handcuffs out of the hospital.

When is a bitch gonna get a break? I thought as I pulled out my phone, texting Derrick's lawyer.

"Aaah..." I sighed from the day's events. "Lord, please protect us all," I said aloud, getting comfortable. It was def going to be a long night.

D.J.

This shit is all my fault. If I would have never touched Pop's gun, my sister wouldn't be laid up in the hospital fighting for her life. Mom had been blowing my phone up, but I didn't answer. I didn't have the courage to let her know it was me who shot my sister, even though it was a mistake. Ever since them Lakeside Boys got smashed, I been feeling like someone was gonna roll up on me at any minute, especially after Glo and his crew drew down on us.

Pops always taught me there was no honor among thieves and nobody was untouchable, men, women or children. So, when the door was pushed open when Derrion went to close it, I quickly jumped off the couch behind her. I didn't see Pops. The only thing I saw was his gun pointed at my sister, and I pulled the trigger several times trying to save her, but I fucked up. The shocked look on Pop's face told the whole story. He had never pulled the trigger, so this bullshit that has happened is all on my head.

For a second, I was stuck when everything unfolded, seeing all that blood coming from my better half, my twin. Me and Derrion were closer than close. She has been here for me since day one. So even though she is my sister, her being my twin is much more special. We've always had an unbreakable bond.

After Desire brought me out of my trance, Pops made me leave his crib. I rode around, trying to clear my mind. I didn't know if within a snap of a finger, I had become a fugitive or not. Deep down knowing my father, he's probably taking the rap, but I couldn't let that shit happen. If this shit played out the way I thought it would, there was only one way I could rectify this situation. If it wasn't for them pussy clots, we wouldn't be in this situation right now. So, with that thought I rode by the projects, sending Brandon a text message, letting him know to meet me at SPI corner store in fifteen minutes. Once I rolled up, I didn't see him, so I pulled out my phone and dialed his number.

"Whoa, nah," he said through the phone.

"Dogg, where the fuck you at?" I asked, getting antsy.

"My nigga, I'm in the store. Why you actin all weird and shit?" he asked, not knowing any of what happened. I guess Killa Kay hadn't put him up on game.

"Aight, I'll explain everything to you once you come out," I said, hanging up.

Not even two minutes later, Brandon was coming out the store.

Beep! I hit the horn once to get his attention.

"What's up, my nigga?" We slapped hands, shoulder bumping. "Damn, mane, fuck wrong with you?" he asked noticing my red eyes.

"My nigga, I don't even know where to start," I said, pulling out the parking lot.

"I hope you ain't sweating them Lakeside niggas. Dogg, everybody talking about the fight. You know that shit all over *Facebook* and anybody with eyes could see you did yo shit. Dude ain't even get a chance to touch you after you served that ass with a right jab," Brandon said, throwing his right fist towards the windshield as if he were me.

"Nah, my nigga, that is the least of my worries. It's—it's my—it's Derrion."

"What the fuck you mean? Them niggas laid hands on my ba—sister?" he said, catching himself from expressing how he felt for her.

B is a good nigga, but he knows the rules. Nobody is to play with her under no circumstances. Plus, there is no reason to rush anything and if he loves and respects her like he has told me plenty of times, she is worth the wait.

"No, my nigga, this shit is deeper than that." I shook my head.

"What the fuck's up?" he asked, giving me his full attention.

"She is in the hospital, mane. She was shot."

"Shot? Mane, no questions asked, we riding tonight. Fuck that! Who the fuck shot her, dogg?" he asked, pulling his gun off his hip, checking his clip.

"Me, it was a mistake, bruh. After we left the school, Desire dropped us off at her and Pop's crib. She left to go pick him up from the police station. She told us to chill, make ourselves comfortable until they got back. Well, that is what we were doing, until we heard somebody rolling up in the driveway. Before Derrion could even get to the door good, there was a crack in the doorway.

"I had no idea my father was on the other side. All I could see was the tip of a gun. As soon as he pushed the door open, I started shooting before my pops could get a shot off. He wasn't expecting us to be on the other side of that door, and I didn't expect the bullets to hit Derrion. Mane, everything happened in slow motion. I just reacted, dogg." After telling my side of what happened, I couldn't do shit but hold my head down, but I quickly picked it back up to keep my eyes on the road.

"So, what you need me to do?" he asked, knowing there is a method to my madness. "You know I got yo back, no matter what," he said with sadness in his voice. He didn't sound as hyped as he was a second ago, knowing it was me. That I was the reason my sister was laid up in the hospital fighting for her life.

"Dogg, I need to get this shit off my chest. I'm ready to ride on those niggas straight up," I said. I knew I needed to take this shit out on somebody. I honestly didn't give a fuck who felt the pain I wanted to dish out, as long as I could get this shit off my chest.

"Say no more. If you rockin, I'm rollin, all day every day."

***

Later that night, Brandon and I were dressed in all-black, ready to ride on them niggas.

"You ready to stop these niggas' clocks, lil bro?"

"Born ready, my nigga," I responded, but truth was I had actually never killed anyone in my life. I then sent a prayer beyond the clouds that my sister wouldn't be the first. *Lord, please don't take her away from us so soon*, I thought.

"I just want you to know D.J., however this shit turns out, I love you. We been through a lot and if I die tonight, just know I have no regrets," he said as he held his fist out for me to bump.

Instead, I took him in my arms and hugged my nigga for what I hoped wasn't the last time. The reality was, I may never see him again and the same for him. I said a quick prayer as we continued to load up our firepower and then headed out the door.

As we were headed towards Lakeside, I could feel my phone vibrate in my pocket. *Damn, I should've left this bitch at home, because it was a big ass distraction.* For the last twenty minutes, somebody was blowing me up. Instead of picking it up, I let it ring because I don't think I could take any more fucked-up news right now. I was already close to the edge, and the only thing left for me to do was jump off the cliff. With one false move, it was sure to happen.

"You good over there, my nigga?" Brandon asked.

"Yeah," I replied, keeping the conversation short.

"Ok, let's move then."

I didn't even realize we had made it to Lakeside. Without having to say another word, we hopped out the dope rental and pulled our ski masks over our faces. Even though I had an "I don't give a fuck" mental, I knew I still had to be cautious. I didn't want to have prison anywhere in my planned future. As we closed in on the front door of Lakeside's trap house, I moved with ease as if I had been going with my move all my life. A nigga was on a mission, I had no room for mistakes.

Neither Brandon nor I had no clue on how many niggas was moving in this bitch, but the move was to leave every nigga in this bitch lying flat. As I stood on one side of the front door Brandon stood on the other making eye contact with one another. I realized that this could actually be the last time we would ever see one another in this life. But fuck it was definitely too late for any regrets. I saw Brandon throw his gloved hand in the air, indicating the countdown.

One. Two. Three. At the same time, we kicked the door down with no effort and without question, squeezed triggers without a second thought. Anything we spotted on the move had been brought to an instant stop, crumbling to the floor like a rag doll. One of the dread heads threw his body behind the couch, but I didn't miss a beat and letting my finger up off the trigger wasn't an option.

"Cover for me!" I heard Brandon shout. I could see out the corner of my eye he had to reload his weapon. As he snapped the clip in his gun, I could see someone coming from the side room with a gun pointed directly at my nigga's head.

"Bitch, put the gun down, pull the muthafuckin trigger and you'll regret it," I said as soon as I creeped behind his ass. Dropping the gun to the floor and throwing his hands in the air, I quickly kicked the gun towards Brandon. "How many more in this bitch?" The tip of my gun rested snuggly on the back of his head. "Oh, bitch, you can't talk?" I asked, slapping him in the head to see if that shit will get some act right.

I thought about all the gangsta stories I heard about my pops and realized the apple definitely didn't fall too far from the tree. *Like father like son*, I assumed.

"My nigga, I think you should speak now or forever hold your peace. I'm not going to ask yo bitch ass no more. Is anybody else in this muthafucka?"

"No," he answered in a thick Jamaican accent.

"Aight, there ain't shit else we got to do then," Brandon said, cocking his gun, placing a bullet in the chamber.

"Wait! Don't kill my dad."

I looked in the direction of the tiny voice of a little boy. As soon as I turned my head, I heard the deafening sound of Brandon's gun being fired and if it wasn't for the black mask pulled over my face to conceal my identity, blood would have been splattered across my face. The little boy stopped dead in his tracks and fell to his knees. In that instant, everything began to move in slow motion and before I realized what was happening, Brandon had stumbled.

"Fuck!" he shouted, grabbing me out of my trance. When I looked to see what happened Brandon had been shot in the leg by some nigga we had chapped out. He still had enough breath in his body to pull the trigger to hit my nigga. I walked over to where the dude was laying and fired one final shot between his eyes.

"We gotta go," I looked over at Brandon as he pulled the mask off his face.

"What the fuck you doing, my nigga?" I asked him, referring to him pulling his mask off.

"Nigga, I can't breathe with this shit on and besides, it ain't like nobody in this bitch to recap what happened."

Without saying a word, I looked over at the little boy who stared at our every move. Brandon's eyes followed the direction where I had set my sights.

"Nah, don't even think about it."

"No witness, no case," Brandon said, just as he raised his arm, pulling the trigger without a second thought.

Yolanda Moore

Jo Jo

It had been about two weeks since a bitch been ducked off, hiding with the rich and famous. Now don't get me wrong, I could get comfortable in any type of weather in the hood, or where I am right now laid up in the lap of luxury. But being here was like a vacation, and even when it poured down raining, the sun shined. I had to get back to my life where all my friends and mostly associates were, especially my bitch, Dirty Diana. I know baby cakes was worried sick. Now that the heat calmed down about the robbery, I knew I was in the clear to go back to where I resided. Besides, I knew the money I had taken had been replaced, because it must have been insured. If not, suffer bitches.

I grabbed my knock off Fendi bag and headed out of the secured area my parents called home. One thing for sure, I will definitely be back. The Southside Projects may be embedded in me but a bitch like me, you can't keep away from a piece of good ole fashion cock. Home boy at the security gate was worth so much more than securing the premises. Like they say, behind every ugly face is some good dick and I promise, I would be back for more.

On my way out the gates of the estates, I blew my new boo a kiss. His face turned fifty shades of red. Of course, he was just like the rest, too good to come his good lovin ass out the closet. I honestly didn't care. I wasn't fucking for a ring. I just laughed and kept it pushing because if he knew like I knew, he would want to partake in my games, unless he wanted the neighbors to know how I had them toes curling last night. What could I say? I not only inherited my mother's good looks and vicious body and giving excellent head didn't fall too far from the tree.

As I drove with the need for speed, I had not noticed the state trooper ducked off on a side road, until it was too late.

"Fuck!" I shouted, hitting the steering wheel as I began to slow down and act as normal as I possibly could. My heart started to race, and if it wasn't for the tight grip I had on the steering wheel, I think I would have lost control of my car. "Girl, calm down, the nigga hadn't even turned on his lights," I said, talking to myself as the trooper rode behind me. I looked down in my lap when my phone started to ring.

In my heart, I knew this was the end for me, but I refused to answer whoever the fuck thought now was a good got damned time to call me. Maybe this was a sign from God letting me have a moment to tell whoever bye, but fuck that. I needed to keep my full undivided attention in this mirror because I swear, I wasn't going out like no sucka. The police would definitely have to kill me. I have heard all the horror stories of what happens to you in prison. Even though I didn't mind at all being a nigga's bitch, I wasn't about to be forced into submission.

Just as that thought crossed my mind, the trooper's lights came flashing, sending my heart racing into overdrive. I had to think quick because I had only two options. One, pull over and let his ass haul me off to prison or two, put the pedal to the metal. Either way I was doomed, so I copped out and settled on pulling over. As the trooper did the same, I realized I wasn't even wearing my fucking seatbelt. So, as inconspicuously as I possibly could, I eased the seatbelt over my shoulder and across my hips. I then placed both hands on the wheel so the officer would not have any reason to shoot me.

Life is too short, especially by the hands of the people are sworn in to protect and serve. When I noticed the trooper's car door swing open, I said a quick prayer and touched my fingers on my forehead, chest and both shoulders to signify the cross.

It was like time seemed to slow down and the first thing I noticed was the trooper's combat boots hit the pavement, taking heed it was a man. That was definitely a plus in my book. Me and bitches just didn't get along, because them conniving tramps felt there wasn't enough dick in this world to go around.

The more time passed by, the more anxious I became, and the more fearfulness took over my wellbeing. I continued to grip the steering wheel not realizing my freshly manicured nails dug into the palms of my hands, but of course that was the least of my worries. As the trooper closed in on me, I was too afraid to turn my neck, so I could face him. So instead, I watched him from my peripheral.

Knock. Knock. Knock.

I heard the tapping on my window, which made me jump and come out of my trance. I rolled the window down so I could hear exactly what it is that he had to say.

"Yes, sir?" I asked, looking at him.

"Where are you in a rush to? And I don't want to hear it is a family emergency," he said.

"Oh, you caught me," I said, laughing it off. "Well, honestly you caught me. I'm actually coming from Cypress Estates, headed to my father's church. He would kill me if I'm late again today," I said, praying my wack ass story worked.

"What church are you speaking of?" he asked, trying to see if he would catch me in a lie.

"Come As You Are Ministry, right outside of Ponchatoula." Thank God there was really a church. I could see the stone-cold look melt off his face a little.

"Pastor John is your father?" he asked with a knowing tone.

"Yes," I said, not knowing if I should smile, cry or rejoice. I just hope ole father dear hadn't given him any problems, but knowing my father, he always tried to portray the man of the cloth, like his undercover gangsta ass didn't know the struggle of robbing, stealing or killing.

"Alrighty then, he is a great guy. He has donated thousands of dollars to the YMCA camp Ponchatoula sponsors every summer for the kids. Pastor John is really a great guy. You know what? Just give me your license and registration and you're free to go. You won't be receiving a speeding ticket today," he said smiling, while I discreetly rolled my damn eyes.

That is just how my father has always been. He's dripped in charisma and lit up a room every time he stepped in with his thousand-dollar Tom Ford suits and red bottom loafers that I might add, the church paid for. Of course, I could see right through his fake Mary Mary's "It's The God in Me" act. Once a snake, you will always lay on your stomach and slither.

Once I handed over my license and registration, he turned to walk back to his state-issued vehicle, I'm pretty sure to run my name. Thank God, a bitch never been to jail and keeps a squeaky-clean record. I pulled my phone out so I could log into my *Facebook* and *Instagram* accounts while the trooper ran my name into his database. I held my phone up just as he was stepping out of his car, so I could take a picture to post. The caption read, "Lock me up please and throw away the key!"

I smiled as I posted, because for the first time since I have been getting interrogated about my speedometer, I just realized how sexy this tall glass of white milk is. I was too busy trying not to get arrested for the damn robbery I committed a few weeks ago. I would have hated to mace his ass and then press the gas, leaving him in my dust. Thank God for big and small favors.

Just as my friends and followers were posting and responding back to what I had posted, I put my phone away because Mr. Officer was headed back into my direction.

"Hey, did everything check out or do you have to arrest me and beat me too?" I asked, which was my way of flirting. All men, in my book, were curious a time or two in their life but always too afraid to jump off the cliff. Well, jump off into me, that is. So, I always gave them courage to do what they've always dreamed about.

"Actually, you are under arrest. Could you step out the car, sir?"

What the fuck happened?

"What the fuck are you arresting me for?" I asked in a more manly voice. Shit had just got real. I pressed on the gas, but only to make the engine roar because my car was in park.

"Do anything stupid besides stepping outside of this car and I'll be forced to take action," he said, pulling his gun and pointing it at my head. I guess all the good shit about my father donating money and all that extra bullshit he was talking went out the window. With his gun trained on me as if he was a sharpshooter, I had no other got damn choice, but to calmly remove myself from the car.

"You are under arrest for outstanding bench warrants for child support," he announced as he slung my pretty ass around, slamming me on the back of my car and cuffing me.

"Child support?" I asked.

That is when it hit me. When I was fourteen years old, I lost my virginity to that no-good cum swallowing, man stealing, pregnant by everybody in the projects including me, trick Meeka. All because my undercover, sexually abusive ass father didn't want nobody to know by the time the sun set instead of fucking his wife, he took the liking in fucking his son instead.

As I was thrown in the back of the trooper's car, my mind couldn't help but wonder to how my ass ended up in this predicament in the first damned place. I guess ole Pastor John stopped paying the child support for the child he created. Even though Meeka's kid was fathered by me, my no-good ass daddy agreed to pay the child support. Now, here I am for whatever reason, being thrown in the back of a police car being treated like Rodney King and hauled off to jail.

The only thing I could think about at the moment, while Officer Dick Head called a tow truck company, was the money from the robbery being in the trunk of my car. As soon as I get processed in the parish, I was demanding my free call so I could hit up Dirty Di to bail a bitch out of the East Baton Rouge Parish Prison.

Meeka

De'riah Makhi London is what I decided to name the new ad-
dition to my family. A bitch was almost running out of names,
I had so many damn kids. I was still a little groggy from all
the medication the doctor doped a bitch up with, but I wasn't
going to complain. It had been nine long miserable months not
being able to have a drink or blunt to calm my damn nerves,
when my bad ass kids ran around the house screaming, jump-
ing on my sofa and fucking shit up like only the project kids
can. Fuck, I didn't expect anything less. I gave my own mother
hell.

I was so fucking bad the bitch called, or shall I say know
as my mom, left me with her mother, so she could do whatever
the fuck she pleased. But see, that is where I drew the line. I
would not dare leave my kids on the next muthafucka so I
could chase dick and catch cum. These bitches could say what
they want, but I already suffer with abandonment issues. I'm
a lot of things like a whore, a homewrecker, you could even
say I am a Section 8, food-stamp-loving bitch. But no one
would not dare open their fucking mouth and say I didn't take
care of my kids. Why? Because it would be a lie from the pits
of hell, words coming straight from my lovely grandmother,
God rest her soul.

I decided to chill and watch some of the hospital's free
cable, while my baby was gone getting different tests run on
her, and also while the doctors and nurses left me the hell
alone. The hospital is supposed to be relaxing, but these
muthafuckas didn't know how to let a bitch rest. Today
though, I was glad to get a little peace of mind, so I turned the
television to my favorite movie network. Yep, *Lifetime*.

Ever since I was a little girl, I loved this sick, wicked ass
shit for two reasons. One, I was always dealing with someone

else's man and two, I had abandonment issues on both my mother and father's side. Watching *Lifetime* always helped me feel better. Did that make just as sick as the people in the movies? I mean, a bitch love someone else that could relate to them, and as a wise muthafucka once said, misery loves company. So, I laid my ass back, got comfortable and ate my gummy bears and drank my apple juice the hospital cafeteria served me.

"Bitch, what the fuck are you doing? Get yo stupid, dumb, white ass out the house, before this white nigga kill yo stupid ass!" I said, yelling at the TV really wishing I could lay hands on this hoe. *For the life of me, I never understood why my ass watches shit like this*, I thought, shaking my head as I watch this muthafucka creep up behind this dumb broad. "I swear to God!" I lay in bed with my fist balled up, watching the TV with intensity.

"A bitch like me would have never given in to his perverted looking ass. White bitches be straight trippin! I would rather be with a broke nigga than to be with a rich one. Niggas think since they money long, they can tell a bitch to jump and expect they ass to respond by asking how high," I said out loud to myself, popping another gummy bear in my mouth. *These lil muthafuckas are good*, I thought.

"How are you, Ms. London?" I heard, right before I could respond to the knock at the door. These hoes don't even give you time to say come in, no privacy.

"I'm good," I said as I continued to look at the TV

"Well, I'm just here to check your vital signs, as usual."

"I should have known," I said when a commercial interrupted my damn movie. Looking up finally at the nurse, she held a small smile on her face she wanted me to interpret as a peace offering. Just as I was about to open my mouth and let some smart-ass remark come out, I spotted a familiar face passing and before I knew it, I shouted her name.

"Desire!" I scared the shit out the nurse but that was the least of my worries. I gave that bitch a look that said, *"Hoe, I'm from the projects, that is what we do. Now try me if you want,"* but she didn't test my gangsta.

"Would you like me to get her?" she asked.

"Please."

"Give me a minute," she said, rushing out.

Not even a minute later, Desire came into my room.

"Hey, what's good, chick?" she asked, smiling at me. Well, her lips spread into a smile, but it failed to reach anywhere else. I understood though. With all the shit her and Derrick was going through, she hasn't had any reason to smile.

"Nothing, my girl. How are you holding up?" I asked her, without asking her what was up with everything that has happened.

"Well, it's obvious everyone knows, huh?" she asked, reaching to give me a hug.

"Yeah, you know social media leaves no stone unturned," I told her as I held my phone up so that she could see it.

"I guess not."

"So, how is she?" I asked about Derrion with a sincere heart.

Even though *Facebook* and the *'Gram* told all, nothing was better than hearing shit right from the horse's mouth.

"She is good and stable, finally. Baby girl really fought a tough fight, and I'm glad she is living to tell the story."

"Did they arrest whoever was responsible for that shit?" Even though rumor was Derrick got interrogated, I know he ain't do no shit like that to his own child. That is just how shit is for a black man, always getting accused of some shit he didn't do, instead of the cops going out and finding the real villain.

"No, girl," she said, keeping it short and sweet. "So, where is this new beautiful baby of yours?"

Before the words could fully roll off her lips, the nurse was bringing De'riah in the room.

"Speaking of there she is, right there," I said, giving that same tight-lipped smile the nurse gave me earlier. Why did this bitch have to bring my baby back right now? I wasn't ready for no one to see her.

"Awww, let me see her." Desire hopped up before I could protest. "She's...she's," Desire stumbled on her words and just as quick as she took my baby into her arms, was just how quick she had given her back to the nurse, making a dash for the door.

Desire

My biggest fear had just become a reality. It was no longer a nightmare. I tried to calm myself down, but I couldn't catch my breath. It felt like all the life was being sucked out of me. *How could my ass be so damned weak-minded?* Here I was playing super mom, super wife, super fuck and super stupid. *I gotta be the dumbest bitch God sent his son to die for.* I had to get the fuck out of this hospital and fast, before I turned into a mad black woman and burned this bitch down to ashes. I briskly walked back to Derrion's room. As soon as I burst through the door, everyone's attention landed on me.

"What the fuck!" Derrick yelled, reaching for his hip to grab his gun. He stormed over to me, jerking my arm. "What the fuck is wrong with you, Desire? Have you lost your fucking mind?" he asked, gripping my arm tight as fuck, but that was the least of my worries.

"I must have lost my mind to ever think a no-good ass dog like you could ever be faithful to me!" I yelled, not giving a fuck who I disturbed.

"Mane, you really delirious right now. So, could you calm the fuck down and tell me what the fuck the problem is? And the shit better be legit, because right now I'm not feeling this insane ass mindset you in."

"First off, get your filthy ass hands off me." I jerked my arm away. "And secondly, all your fucking answers to your questions are in room 208," I said, grabbing my purse. "How fucking convenient." I looked back at Derrick before slamming the door.

Once I got outside in the cool crisp air, I was sucked into the darkness of night. I hit the start button on my key ring to start the new car Derrick bought me, right after we moved into our new home. Now I see why his ass had been so generous with all the gifts. What? He thought he could just wine and dine my ass and everything would be alright? Right game, wrong bitch. For the life of me, I just don't understand how these no-good ass niggas always complain about how a woman was a no-good hoe ass bitch, who fucked and sucked every nigga round town, but those are the first cum-catching hoes they run to. I could not even be mad at neither of them though, only myself. Some niggas will always be hoes and a no-good, back-stabbing ass bitch will always be there to stab you in the back, no matter how good you are to them.

Buying food stamps my ass, Derrick was paying for more than her EBT card. *How could I be so damn stupid*, I thought as I pulled up at home. Once I got inside, I immediately began pulling off my clothes, leaving a trail behind me. I walked naked to the kitchen to fix me a glass of wine and then proceeded to the bathroom to take a much-needed hot bath. Ever since all this shit been going on, I haven't been taking care of me and honestly, it was ok because when you care deeply about others, that is what you do. But Derrick fucking another bitch is the thanks I get.

I ran a tub full of hot water and turned *Pandora* on to listen to some soothing music to pacify my broken heart. My phone started ringing, interrupting my peace. I looked down at the screen, noticing it was Derrick still blowing my phone up. I programmed his number under "restricted" and continued on my way to the hot water that awaited.

"Aww," a moan escaped my mouth as I stepped my aching body inside the burning water. My body welcomed the discomfort, because just for a split second, it distracted the hurt that my heart felt. Only for a second though.

As my mind wandered, I laid back in the tub getting as comfortable as possible, sipping my wine straight from the bottle, fuck the cup. Drinking, I listened to Anthony

Hamilton's, "Her Heart." Did this nigga really think I was fucking stupid? How could he do this to me? I needed to get the fuck from around him. No way did my house feel like a home anymore. In a snap of a finger, shit took a turn for the worse.

I must have dozed off, because when I opened my eyes, the first thing I spotted was the wine bottle floating in the tub with me. The water had also turned ice cold and my fingers and toes were like prunes. Instead of running more water I stepped out, draping myself with a towel and grabbed my phone before I headed to our bedroom. Not even giving a fuck if someone called or not, I decided to not check missed phone calls or text message and powered my phone off.

I really didn't care if I didn't hear from a soul. My only concern at the moment was to figure out my next move, because sleeping in the same bed under the same roof was out the got damn question. For now, I'm just resting my damn nerves. It is passed one o'clock in the morning and the only thing was open was a bitch's legs. At the moment, all I wanted to do was sleep this alcohol off and let tomorrow worry about itself.

The next morning, I woke up with an excruciating headache. I didn't even want to move, but the sun was shining bright as fuck in my face. I took that as a sign from God and got my ass up, even though my body was telling me something different. Plus, no matter how much I pretended to be asleep, I know sleeping would not wash away my problems. After brushing my teeth and washing my face, I proceeded to the kitchen to fix myself something to eat. I settled for a few slices of toast bread to soak up the remaining alcohol on my stomach from last night.

For the first time since being home, I noticed the pile of mail laid in front of the door. Neither Derrick nor I have been home long enough to do anything. So, I walked over bent down and gathered the mail on the floor.

"Let's see," I said as I walked back to the kitchen table to go through the mail. Junk, bullshit, bills, which I don't give a fuck about," I said aloud. All this shit overnight had become the least of my worries. "Why the fuck is this nigga still sending checks?" I became angry at my father. Did he think it was a joke when I said I didn't want shit to do with him?

Wait, I could use this money to get my own place. Fuck it, why not? I didn't have shit. I wanted the fuck out of Derrick's house and with the money my dad had been sending me over the years, I have a few thousand from him I never touched. Yeah, that is exactly what I will do. Like Meeka said months ago, everybody didn't have what I have. A father, especially one that looks out. I didn't have to live how I lived. I chose to stick it out with this nigga and look where it got me. The only thing I gained was a wet ass and a broken heart. Here it is, I damn near was begging this fool to have a baby with me, and his no-good ass dropping off cum like a chicken drops eggs. I had to get out of this situation and fast.

Going back into my room, I got dressed, grabbed my phone and keys and headed out the door. The first thing I noticed when I opened the door was blood. Even though we had a few cleaners come out to clean, I could still see blood. Maybe it was a figment of my imagination because of the trauma we had been through. Nobody had gone through more pain than D.J. and Derrion, but above all, Derrion. Poor baby. They are the only two that would make it hard for me to leave, but I couldn't stay. It was hard, but I know I could still be here for them, without actually being here. I took a deep breath as I powered on my phone and got in my car and took off.

124

Derrick

What the fuck have I gotten myself into? Right after Desire stormed out on some theatrical bullshit, I went down to room 208 just to see what the fuck she was all unruly about. As soon as I stepped into the room and laid eyes on Meeka's baby, there was no doubt in my mind she was mine. Even if I didn't want to lay claim, I couldn't even pretend she wasn't my baby.

"What the fuck you looking at? Are you just going to stand there looking like you have seen a ghost?" Meeka asked as soon as I stepped in the door, like she was expecting me.

"Why the fuck you didn't tell me? And was you intentionally trying to break up my happy home?" I asked with anger in my voice, expecting the hospital staff to come and make me leave.

"Boy, bye! Happy? If you were so happy, why the fuck was you sneaking to my fucking bed every night to come fuck me? And don't stand there all accusingly, because I didn't make her on my fucking own. Every time you came over to blow my back out, you never worried about pulling out! What the fuck you thought was going to happen? So, miss me with them pill head games."

And just like that, the bitch read me my rights, but I didn't give a fuck about any of that shit she was talking at the moment. Here I was, praying over my daughter that she pulled through this horrible ordeal. Protecting my son from receiving a life sentence, losing my bitch and now finding out I got another muthafuckin mouth to feed, almost sent me over the edge. I been blowing up Desire's phone and she kept sending me to voicemail. Did this bitch not know I would kill her fucking ass if she played with me? On second thought, she knew exactly what I'm capable of so, I'ma just give her time to come around. Besides, she had nowhere to go and I was all she had. I decided to give her a minute to gather herself, because right now, I had more demanding shit on my plate. I needed to find my son for one, because the shit I was hearing from the streets was not pretty, and everything I was trying not to expose them to was unfolding right before my eyes. Anyone who had ties to the Southside Projects was bound to get sucked right into the black hole it was.

As for Meeka, that shit was dead. The bitch pussy wasn't even good, it was just convenient, nothing to run and call home about. The only other reason I kept in close contact with her no-good ass was because I must admit, the hoe could cook some fya ass dope. That bitch was every dope boy's dream when it came to whipping her wrist. So, from now on, shit between us was strictly business. Nothing with us will ever be pleasurable.

"Hello, I'm Doctor Williams, I have some great news for you guys," a different doctor than the one we've been dealing with said as she stepped through the door.

"The only great news you could give us is clearance, and to also assure me my baby girl will be ok in the long run," I said, getting straight to the point. Fuck the small talk.

"Actually, that is all correct. I am here with her release papers. She has done nothing but progress in the two weeks she's been here. As for being ok in the long run, I attest to that. As long as she makes it to every physical therapy session, she will be up and at 'em in no time."

As each word rolled off her tongue, I was overjoyed with the news. I said a quick salute to the creator for sparing my baby girl.

***

"Derri, you ready to roll?" Keisha asked as I gathered all her stuff to take down to the car.

"Give me a lil minute, Keish. I'm going to grab the car and I'll be back up to gather her," I said, kissing the top of Derrion's head.

On my way down, I tried calling D.J. for the umpteenth time. He still hadn't answered and if he didn't soon, I was going to fuck his ass clean up when I saw him. I was worried my son went off the deep end. Especially with him having the same personality as me. I also worried for him because I knew how cold the streets could be. The streets would chew you up and spit you out. It didn't matter about your age, race or gender, anybody could get it. So, once I got my baby girl settled, I was sending out my own type of Amber Alert and gathering a team of my niggas to go on a manhunt.

As soon as we pulled up in Keisha's driveway, I carefully picked my baby girl up and walked her to the door, while Keisha unlocked it. Instead of walking her to her room, I headed straight to the guest room. While she was laid up in the hospital, I had the guest room turned into a mini hospital, just in case.

"Poppa, you didn't have to do all this, you know. I'm ok," she smiled as I laid her in the bed.

"That is not true, princess, I gotta do whatever it takes to make sure you have everything your little heart desires. Plus, I wanna make it hard on these lil niggas, I'ma have to kill once they start running behind you," I said, rubbing her head.

"Start?" She looked at me like, *are you serious?* "I have the boys going crazy," she laughed, trying to fuck with me.

"I swear, on everything I love, I better not catch any of these lil knucklehead ass niggas looking at you," I said, kissing her forehead.

"Poppa, I do remember what happened. I know who shot me, but of course I pretended I lost my memory. Could you please forgive D.J.? I have, because I know it was an accident. That's my brother, my best friend, and I'm my brother's keeper. That is something you have always taught us. I really haven't said much since all this happened because I could never hate D.J., even if everyone has turned their back on him."

Derrion held her head down after she finished speaking and the shit cut me like a knife.

"Baby girl, listen to me." I pulled her head up by her chin so she could look me in the eyes. "There ain't nobody that has walked this earth I care about more than my children. Yes, I do know what D.J. did was a mistake and I would never disown him, because he would lay his life down for you and not do damage by taking it away. I have always been honest with both of y'all, even though I have tried to shield y'all from the life I live and away from the projects. It is my job to love, protect and to provide and I plan on doing that. So, no worries, baby girl. All is well," I said, kissing the top of her head once more. "I love you, now get you some rest. I will be back later. I need to go find your brother."

Without a doubt in my mind, I felt shit would get worse than it was before it got better. I just prayed in the long run, nothing more would happen to my children.

***

"What it do?" Killa Kay asked as I hopped out my whip in front of the projects, leaving my door open.

"Mane, I'm cooling. What's good with you, big homie? I wanted to thank you the other day for coming through for me.

Dogg, you and Lunch saved my daughter's life, man. I owe you, nigga," I said, giving him a G-hug.

"Nah, big homie, no debts this way. I know if the shoe was on the other foot, I could count on you to have my mutha-fuckin back in a situation like that. So, it's all gravy. Besides what's that saying, as long as I owe you, I'll never be broke?" we both laughed.

"Look, my nigga, I'm trying to catch up with D.J. Have you seen him? That lil nigga ain't picking up and I would hate to think something is wrong with my baby boy, because nigga's gone bleed if a hair is out of place on his head, ya feel me?"

"G-shit, lil homie been ducked off over here with my lil bro, ya feel me? And you know ain't no nigga bold enough to come in these projects and fuck nothing up. Besides, you don't take it out on him too much, my nigga. Lil homie reminds me so much of you and each day, the lil nigga turning into a beast." I walked off without further acknowledging what Killa Kay was saying.

For one, I didn't need no nigga telling me how easy to take it on my son. My people or not, I didn't respect the fact that he don't take care of his own children, so I definitely wasn't hearing that shit on how to take care of mine. When it came to fatherhood, we viewed shit on two different levels.

As I strolled toward the rear of the projects, I spotted Meeka coming out of her apartment. Lil momma was defi-nitely shaking back from the baby. *My baby, damn.* I made mental note to get a DNA test on the kid. I already knew the answer though, it looked just like me but fuck that, you can never be to sho' when it came to a bitch from the projects. For now, though I kept it pushing because I was on a mission.

Without even knocking, I bust through Killa Kay and Brandon's Gram's shit like she was my Grams. Like I lived at that muthafucka and paid rent, I headed straight for Brandon's room.

"Why the fuck…" I stopped mid-sentence. My son was on the bed fucking some lil broad.

"Damn, Pops, fuck!" He hurried to get dressed once he noticed it was me, as the lil girl he was sexing pulled the sheets over her body to hide herself. I turned my back to give them a moment. A few minutes later, D.J. was walking past me, still fixing his clothes. On some shit, I wanted to dap my lil nigga down because I honestly never thought he was fucking. And, as far as I could see, it was too late for us to be having the talk.

"Pops, before you say anything, it wasn't what it looked like."

"Nigga, this shit is bigger than Nino Brown," I said, wrapping my hand around the back of his neck, pushing him into the kitchen for a little more privacy. "Here I am worried about yo lil knucklehead ass, and you over here probably getting more pussy than me."

"Pops, I doubt anybody getting mo' pus…" I gave him a look, daring him to say it, true or not.

"Look, son, shit is hot right now and I don't…"
Boom. Boom. Boom.

Before I could get my full sentence out, I dove towards my son as we both crashed to the floor. I used my body to cover him in all the madness that popped off within seconds. *Who the fuck could that be?* It was like bullets were flying directly at this apartment. Now don't get me wrong, muthafuckas stay shooting in the projects, but niggas know not to play with Killa Kay and Brandon's Grams, so it had to be somebody with a death wish.

"Pops, get off me! I gotta go protect my girl. She carrying my seed!" I could hear my son yelling over the ruckus.

Seed? I thought. What the fuck! I didn't play with the thought too long though, because we were all in a life-or-death situation. So, I pulled my Glock off my hip and covered for my son.

"Nigga, go handle yo business," I yelled as he took off to the room he had just came from.

Where the fuck was my niggas when I needed them? As soon as that thought crossed my mind, D.J. came back out the room, bustin his gun like he been smashing shit. Now wasn't the time for me to figure that shit out either, so I kept shooting until we're sure the nigga, or them niggas was gone.

Yolanda Moore

D.J.

Brandon's grams, Ms. Chainy's, funeral was full of grief-stricken mourners. Family and friends were left with wet faces and a broken heart. Damn near the whole Southside Projects was in attendance and the patrons had the church house looking like a fashion show. Even I decided to wear a customized Tom Ford suit and trench coat. The color scheme was red, black and white in honor of Ms. Chainy, because we were all ready to paint the town red for this senseless murder committed on one of our own.

Even though this was a time of sorrow, I had to hold it together and be strong for my nigga Brandon. I could only imagine what he was feeling and mentally going through. My nigga has been there for me every time I have needed him, and I'm prepared to do the same.

Looking around the church from the front sitting with the Chainy family, I spotted my father. We locked eyes and I couldn't break our stare. I knew he had so many questions. For starters, when did I learn to aim and shoot? Where did I get the gun and lastly, when was I going to let him know I am becoming a father in a few months? All that shit was dropped on him at once, without us not even having one conversation. But what the fuck was I to say? "Hey, Pops! Congrats, you will soon be a grandfather. Oh, and by the way, I killed a couple of them Jamaican niggas off Lakeside."

Nah, I couldn't do that. I could only imagine how he wanted to kill my ass. One thing my father has always done is try to keep us separate from his lifestyle, and he was more of a "do as I say, not as I do" type of dude, but the shit was inevitable. Unavailable as long as he held ties with the Southside Projects, we were going to be bound someway, somehow.

Finally turning back to the preacher proclaiming how great of a woman Ms. Chainy, was my mind began to wander. I'm so grateful I didn't lose my sister. After everything settled down after the hit on our lives, Pops told me Derrion was worried about me, she forgave me and knew me shooting her was a mistake. She wanted to see me. I needed to see her. So, right after the service, I was going no if's and or buts about it. My twin was my lifeline and if I had lost her, I don't know what the fuck I would have done. Maybe lost my mind.

After the funeral service, we all prepared to go to the gravesite letting the family walk out first, me included. To the naked eye, you would never know underneath our trench coats we also wore artillery of our choice. I decided on an AK-47, some big boy shit. Like I said, we leaving blood, bodies and brains for the boys in blue to play detective, instead of harassing muthafuckas out here trying to make a living.

As I walked out the church double doors, I was hit with sunshine but was surprised to see it raining. I have grown up to know that as the devil beating his wife, which could only mean one thing. *No telling how the day would go*, I thought shaking my head. Just when I had that thought, out the corner of my eye, I saw sudden movement. I don't know why I ducked down, but my inner voice told me to do so.

"Watch out!" I shouted as I collided with my baby momma, forcing her to the ground. Just as we hit the pavement, the window inside one of the double doors shattered on our heads. Instantly my survival streak kicked in. Beyonca army-crawled back into the church for safety and as far as I could tell, she hadn't been touched. Good. I quickly made the symbol of the cross, said a quick prayer, coming out my trench coat swiftly with my AK.

Across the street, I spotted some niggas with dreads, which let me know them boys were Lakeside. Thank God, I could tell them niggas apart, because I was sick of this shit and was ready to touch anything against the gang. I let my AK spit with no remorse. I dared these niggas to come around again, disrespecting my set. It was already bad enough these niggas killed Ms. Chainy, but to let them disrespect her by spitting on her grave, was sending me on a whole 'nother level.

Boom. Boom. Boom.

Brandon stood beside me bustin his shit, ready to body sum'.

Boom. Boom. Boom.

Shots were fired back at us, so we took cover behind somebody's car and just in time too, because the window of the car shattered where I was just standing. *Damn.*

"One, two, three..." I counted, anticipating my next move. "You ready, bro?" I asked Brandon.

He simply gave me a head nod and that was all the indication I needed. Before I decided to go with my move, I looked under the car and saw a set of feet moving towards us. I knew to look, because the moment of mayhem turned to a moment of silence, which let me know them niggas was creeping. I placed my finger over my mouth, indicating silence and my trigger finger for him to shoot the nigga in the foot.

Boom.

"Fuck!" I heard the opps yell.

We had caught him off guard. Good. As soon as we hopped up to go smash his ass, in the distance I could hear police sirens, so I knew we needed to move quick. I also heard the scream of tires.

"Bitch, I'ma skip the small talk and not even worry myself about who sent you. What them niggas should have let you know, you fuckin with the wrong niggas. We do this shit!" Brandon said calmly as he raised his gun, putting a bullet hole right in the middle of the Jamaican's eyes. His head flew back and the nigga was dead before his head touched the ground.

"Ayo, y'all, we gotta get the fuck outta here!" one of my lil homies from the projects said, bringing us out of kill zone. Before we took off, Brandon turned and put three more slugs in the Rasta's face. We both climbed in the back seat of my pop's car. In the distance, I could tell the cops were closer than we thought. My pops put the car in drive. Not even five minutes into the drive, we were bypassing the police. We all remained calm as if we were not the muthafuckas they were in search of.

Meeka

How dare this nigga to ask me for a muthafuckin blood test! His bitch ass wasn't worried about fucking me raw, now he's convinced my baby isn't his? I swear to God, I don't know what kind of luck I have with these niggas! I'ma give him what he wants though, if that's how he wants to play me like I'm just some trick ass hoe? Well, maybe I am, but that don't give his ass the right to treat me as such. I hit the blunt hard as a muthafucka, holding it to the side, taking a look at it before I kissed it.

"Lawd, am I happy to not be pregnant no more," I said aloud to myself.

I could feel my eyes get heavier by the second. No lie, that nigga Scrappy be having some fya ass weed. I know the nigga be stealing the shit from Ms. Ethel. That old bitch keep a stash of that good shit. I know Ms. Ethel got her shit from Derrick's no-good ass, and that nigga only smokes the best. Yeah, I could've called and begged his ass, but Derrick is as stubborn as a mule. So, me calling him would have been a waste of time. I had to make a sacrifice by giving Scrappy's dope-head ass a hand job because fucking him was out of the picture. I can't say I'm the best person in the world, but this pussy here didn't fuck muthafuckas that sucked on glass dick.

Speaking of dick, I hadn't had any in a little minute and this fucking weed only made me want some dick even more. I had been a good girl and followed the doctor's orders by not even looking at a dick for the last six weeks. *Now was a whole 'nother story*, I thought as I slid my fingers of my weed-free hand down into my pink boy shorts. There was total silence in my apartment. Thank God school was back in session, and the baby was at my cousin's house. A bitch needed a break and I planned to spend my little vacay getting high and fucking, even if that meant I would have to fuck myself. Trust me when I say I knew how to please myself. With my hands where they needed to be, I spread my legs as wide as I needed, scooting to the edge of the couch so I could run my middle finger to my sticky slit, giving myself a lubricant. My pussy was soft and smooth as cream.

"Ooooo yesss!" I rode my fingers, hitting the weed as I felt my heart rate speed up. "Fuck," I yelled, breathing hard. "Get that shit, bitch. Oh, my…" I couldn't take it, but I wasn't about to stop either. I was gonna get this nut one way or another. My fingers moved quick across my clit, like a rockstar playing a guitar on a Friday night live concert. Just as I was about to catch my nut, my fucking phone started to ring, breaking my concentration.

I looked at the time on the wall and knew it wasn't time for my kids to come home, so I ignored the ringing and continued to focus on the task at hand literally. Getting back into the swing of things wasn't hard at all. In fact, my legs began to tremble like an earthquake and the next thing I knew, my cream was sliding down the crack of my ass.

After catching my breath, my damn phone was still fucking ringing and even though I wanted to toss that muthafucka out the door, I decided to answer instead. It was apparent someone was really trying to get in touch with me.

"Hello!" I said with an attitude. *Damn, a bitch can never get a little peace and quiet around this muthafucka.*

"You have a collect ca…" Before the operator could announce who was calling, I was accepting the call. I knew it was Rico, my lil boo from the state pen. He be poppin a bitch off for a little phone sex, and a couple of visits to bring my fine ass up that road to drop off a package.

"Hey, boo!" I said excitedly, "you had a bitch thinking you had left. Either that, or you took a trip to the hole," I said, laughing all sexy and shit.

"Bitch, get yo life. This is yo baby momma, hoe," Jo Jo said laughing.

"Bitch, what the fuck you doing in there? Oh, my God!"

Even though Jo Jo liked dick just as much as me, if not more, we had a child together. My oldest, thanks to his fake ass preaching, tricking father of his. I wasn't mad though, because his tithe-collecting self pays child support on time. Yes, I said child support. See, Jo Jo and I both knew the truth to the scandal we created. Everyone was too afraid to speak the truth about what went down back in the day, except for me that is. Which is why I get a fat ass check monthly to hold the man of the cloth's secret. And as long as he keep a bitch paid, he can always trust his secret is safe with me.

My firstborn was actually for Pastor John and not his son. See, back in the day when my mom was selling pussy to buy dope, our apartment used to be booming with all types of men, running through our shit to get a taste of Candy. But then after a while, her candy wasn't so sweet. That is when I realized that I was in trouble. A few of the men began to look at my young body with a twinkle in their eye as if the sun shined upon me and set as well.

At first, I didn't think much of it. I mean, I have never had the affection of a father, and I had to admit at the moment I loved the attention. Gifts began to come plentiful. Like my cup had started to overflow abundantly. I had all the latest gear, our water and lights stayed on, which meant I didn't have to walk around filthy because I was too ashamed to go by somebody else's house to take a bath. That included my Momo's house too, but that was all my mother's fault. God forbid, I let Momo in our business because if I did, that was a for sure ass beating that would leave me not being able to even sit down. I had also started putting a little weight on, in all the right places though, because a bitch was able to eat breakfast, lunch and dinner. I no longer had to go to school just to get a meal. I was feeling like *The Jeffersons*, and we were moving on up just like they were. I loved my life, and it was all because of the good ole pastor.

Back then, I was too naïve and thought he was poppin it off, because the nigga had a heart for my struggle. Nope, I was wrong. He had shown me life was not like a box of chocolate but far from it. The night I lost my virginity was the night everything changed for me, and as for my mother, she no longer had to wake up dope sick. She didn't care, all that mattered was that her next fix was fa sho. That first week of sex consisted of oral sex. I guess that was his way to bait me in and that he did. By the next week, he had turned my young ass into a sex fiend.

My mother and I both were addicts but from two different sides of the spectrum. Sex and money had become my demon and I was ok with that. I started branching out, spreading my wings. I loved to feel wanted and that feeling alone trumped all.

John started to get jealous, and the tables had turned. He was like putty in my hands. Even though I was going against the grain as he put it, I wasn't in denial about the love I had for him. I mean fuck, he was my first everything, including the first to break my heart. A few months after us fucking and sucking one another, I ended up pregnant with my first child. I was eager to tell John the good news and could not wait until he came to pick me up for one of our excursions.

Under my white mini skirt and tank, I wore his favorite red, lace panty and bra set. I spritzed my body down with Madagascar Vanilla from Bath & Body Works after rubbing my chunky legs down with the matching body butter. I was lit and definitely on go. Once he pulled up, I was done getting myself together. Before we left to go to our usual spot, he made sure to pop my mom off. Always keeping her happy gave us the ability to do as we pleased.

"John."

"What's up, baby girl?" he asked smiling, removing his hand off my thigh to turn down the fully equipped system which played "Whatever You Want," by Tony! Toni! Tone!

"Uh, I have something I wanted to tell you," I said, twirling my thumbs around one another.

"What is it, honey? You know you can tell daddy anything, right?" he asked, placing his big strong hand back to his favorite spot whenever I rode shotgun.

"I'm pregnant," I said abruptly as my heart felt like it would stop at any minute.

Scurr...he slammed on his brakes, pulling to the side of the road before he ran off it.

"What the fuck you just said?" He looked over at me, no longer talking about, honey this or honey that. I didn't even bother opening my mouth to answer his question. It was a rhetorical question. He heard my words loud and clear. I mean, he should have known when he asked me how did my pussy get ten times better overnight? I'm just saying. It has been affirmed pregnant pussy is the best pussy and isn't just a myth. For a minute he just looked at me and the cat had both of our tongues.

That was until he said, "You gotta get rid of it. We can get yo moms cleaned up for a few hours, and I will give her a little something after, ya know?"

"Are you serious right now?" I yelled as tears brewed on the surface, threatening to fall from the threshold of my eyes.

"Yeah, baby, my wife—"

"Nigga, yo wife? Was you fucking thinking about your marriage, when you was fucking the dog shit out of my young ass?" I yelled, simmering on the inside.

"But you knew," he yelled back and that sent my young ass over the edge.

Smack. I slapped the hell out of his ass literally, because after the worst night of my life, I had created a more hideous monster better known as Pastor John.

"Hellooo! Bitch, can you hear me, or are you too damn high to concentrate on what I'm saying?" I heard Jo Jo yell, bringing me out of my daydream.

"Yeah, bitch, I'm here. I heard everything you said. Call ya pops get the nigga to come bond you out, even if I gotta pop him off and if I do, you get a bag for me when you do touch."

"You have one minute left," the operator chimed in, letting us know our conversation would soon come to an end.

"Alright, bitch, don't let me down because if I don't get out of here, these niggas gone take my v-card," Jo Jo said, right before the phone call ended. But if it hadn't, I would've told his ass he lost that shit a long time ago, thanks to his father trying to cover his disgraceful tracks. Now here it was, years later and I was placed on a quest to conquer the belly of the beast.

Desire

When I left Derrick's house, I left everything. I didn't want anything from him, including the car he gave me. A few days after leaving him, I got a friend to follow me back so that I could drop his car back off to him. I knew exactly why Derrick felt the need to treat me the way he did, even if it was behind my back. He sensed I needed him, but the truth was, I didn't. Even though I parted ways from my father on a bad tip, he had not raised a fool. And as my grandmother used to say, it's ok to be a fool, but being someone's damn fool would be outright ridiculous, and I was neither here nor there.

Over the years, my dad had always done what he was supposed to do as a father, being the provider of his household even if I did neglect him. Each month he continued to send me a monthly check I was certain I would never use. They say to never say never, because your words will always come back to bite you in the ass. In my case, my bite was a good one.

The day I left Derrick's house and didn't look back, I went to a hotel and for like a month strong, I had slowly turned the place into my own, until my money started to run low. I didn't have a job, no experience and by then, no car because I took my stupid ass back and dropped it off in the heat of the moment. But I was only following my heart because I refused to be that nigga's doormat any longer than I already have. It didn't take me long to realize I had made a mistake, especially when I had to make a decision whether I should pay for another night in the hotel or feed my stomach. I knew then I had to do something.

I tucked my tail and called an old friend from my neighborhood, because it was clear I had not only washed my hands with my father, but everyone from my past as well. Mike had come through for me and didn't hesitate when I called on him.

He was my high school sweetheart and confessed he had never stopped loving me.

"Morning, my baby, how are you feeling?" Mike asked me because I had been throwing up for the last few days.

"I'm good," I said smiling, but that changed as soon as I sat up in the bed. I pushed him out of my way and ran to the bathroom in time to throw up all over the seat as Mike held my hair.

"Listen, I don't know if this is a good time to tell you, but my mom thinks you might be pregnant and so do I," he said as I looked at him, giving him the evil eye.

"No way am I pregnant," I said, becoming defensive.

"Hey, don't shoot the messenger you know my mother is the best doctor in town and plus, you are showing all the signs, baby," Mike said, taking a seat beside me and the toilet as he held my hand.

I started crying so hard within a snap of a finger, and I could not decipher whether my tears were tears of joy or sorrow. For so long, all I have ever wanted was a family and whenever I was trying, I could not become pregnant for anything in the world. Now here I am, nowhere to actually call home, no income coming in and I could not tell you if my baby is Mike's or Derrick's. From the outside looking in, I know someone that didn't know or understand my situation would label me a whore. But I was far from it. I just decided to give someone my heart that didn't rightfully deserve what I was giving.

"Baby, don't cry," Mike said, brushing my hair off my face, kissing my head like my father used to. That is exactly what I loved about Mike. He was so caring and affectionate. "Whatever way things may fall into place, I am going to always be here for you and our baby, even if he or she isn't mine. We will prevail." He smiled at me and when I tell you if I wasn't in love before, I sure was at that moment.

"I couldn't ask you to take on that responsibility if it isn't yours to take on," I sniffed, also willing myself not to drop another tear.

"I can and I will, sweetheart. Now take this pregnancy test, I'm tired of being in suspense," he said, handing me the pregnancy test as he got up to leave. "I'm going to fix you some breakfast, so after you wash up come meet me in the kitchen." He bent down to kiss me, but I turned my head.

"No, I have to brush my teeth, baby," I smiled, whining.

"I know but I love you and your stinky, throw-up breath," he said, kissing me anyway.

After Mike left to start breakfast, I wasted no time taking the pregnancy test and set the timer on my Fitbit for five minutes. Within that time frame, I brushed my teeth, washed my face and combed my hair, placing it in a messy bun on the top of my head with soft baby hairs framing my face. Finished, and so was the pregnancy test. I looked down and saw I was indeed pregnant. I smiled and walked to the kitchen to give my man the news that in about nine months, we were due to become parents. I had to trust in the Lord that through Christ all things are possible, even the new man in my life who is agreeing to take on a child that may or may not be his.

Rejuvenated, refreshed, renovated and revitalized were the words to describe how I was feeling. After delivering the news to Mike that I was in fact pregnant, we decided to skip the food he took his time to cook and opted to have each other instead. My life turned for the better and I began to believe at the end of each storm will be a rainbow. And boy, was my rainbow colorful.

***

"Ma'am, how are you? Is there anything I can help you with today?" an employee asked as soon as I stepped inside The Children's Place. I turned toward the voice of the worker who was speaking to me. I noticed how she looked down at my flat stomach, maybe wondering if I was shopping for myself, or someone with a child.

"Huh, actually no. I'm ok, thank you for your help though. If I may need you then I'll find you," I replied as politely as possible.

When we departed, we both proceeded to go on about our business. There was so much to pick from throughout the store and I just had to keep in mind to only shop for the basics like onesies, baby blankets and unisex clothing items. I definitely had baby fever. By the time I finished up and made my way to the counter, my items came up to a total of twelve hundred thirty-six dollars and fifty-two cents.

"Will that be all today, ma'am?" the cashier whose name tag read Tiffany B. asked, with a smile plastered on her face.

"Yeah, thank you," I said, reaching inside my purse for Mike's black card that he had given me this morning to do whatever would make me feel better. When it came to him and his mom, the apple didn't fall from the tree. Their family consisted of a long line of doctors and lawyers.

"Look at what the fuck the cat done drug in," I heard behind me closer than anyone should be unless they were fucking. And I had already got my back blown out this morning and knew the voice didn't belong to the dick that fucked me righteously, but I know exactly who it suited. A bum bitch right out the Southside Projects. Tameeka, best known as Meeka, the good dick pleaser. I turned around slowly.

"Bitch, how dare you approach me like I'm some bum bitch! You food stamp auctioning, selling pussy and doing hair out the same Section 8 housing unit ass, bitch." I couldn't stop, this bitch had me on a roll.

"Girl, bye! You just irate because this food stamp selling bitch was having your man." She laughed in my face as if she was at a comedy show.

"You know what? I'm seriously trying to stop from laughing at you, because it definitely won't be with you, sis. Are you hearing this circus clown?" I asked, turning around looking at Tiffany B. as if we had come together. I turned back around, giving this bitch my undivided attention. "It was clear I made a good decision on wearing my messy bun today, so if you don't want to go for what yo project ass know, then you need to clear me because bitch, I stay strapped like laces."

"Bitch, you just caught me at the wrong muthafuckin time because a bitch ain't tryna hit that parish, especially with this open charge I got over my head."

That was all I needed to hear this how wasn't trying to put in no work, so I grabbed my bags and Mark's black card, tucking it safely back into my purse. I walked past her ratchet ass while shoulder bumping that bitch out my way.

"Oh, Tiff, you might want to check lil momma purse. That open charge the bitch got is for shoplifting." I winked at Meeka, smiled and walked out with shopping bags that cost more than that hoe's rent in a year, for my baby that hadn't even become fully developed.

Yolanda Moore

Glo

A dope fiend will always be loyal to his next hit. In the game, that should be the first thing you learn when you are introduced to the streets. Which is why I am slowly but surely closing in on them Southside Project pussies. Thanks to Scrappy, the project dope fiend. As I said, convincing him wasn't hard, all it took was an eight ball to play on Lakeside's side of the field. I also been kicking it with this bitch, Meeka, Scrappy also hooked that up. Did I mention a hoe was only faithful to a dollar? So, to get both of them on a nigga's team was like taking candy from a baby, a piece of cake.

Speaking of, I was enroute to go pick ol girl up. She told me to meet her around the corner at the SPI store off Government Street. I agreed, because she knew it would be a straight warzone if I pulled up to pick off one of their own. I have never been suicidal, and I wasn't about to make any false moves now.

As soon as I pulled up, I spotted lil momma instantly. I hadn't actually met her personally, but we had spoken on the phone a few times, *FaceTimed* and I also checked out her *Instagram* page. I stepped outside of my car, adjusting my Glock on my hip, leaned back on my car and folded my arms all cool like as I watched Meeka swish her thick hips my way. I wondered if that fat pussy was as juicy as it looked and not a misprint. Hopefully, I wouldn't have to speculate much longer.

"Hey sup, boo?" She hugged me, placing a kiss to the side of my mouth.

I gripped that small ass waist of hers once she leaned into me, as I imagined fucking some shit up. I hated to say, but if she meant anything to Derrick, it was definitely that nigga's loss. Not wanting to be in the area too much longer we got in the car and sped off.

"So, where we headed?" she asked me, licking them sexy ass lips.

"You like Caribbean food?"

"Yeah, sure."

"Aight then, we about to head to one of my favorite Jamaican spots. They serve the best food, so you're going to love it."

"Is that a promise?" she asked me seductively.

"Fucking right. We only serve the best," I said, meaning an assortment of things.

For the rest of the drive, we listened to some soft R & B without further communication. It took us forty-five minutes to make it across town. I didn't tell her, but I had someone meeting me there. I needed to check on a lil something that couldn't wait.

"Sup with it?" my cousin Kingston asked me as soon as I walked in the spot.

"Shit, I'm chillin, potna. Everything is everything. How's the business doing?"

"Definitely can't complain, boi. We're doing numbers. We eating like the kings we were born to be," he said, referring to my real business. Glo's Caribbean Food was just a front for what we were actually pushing.

"So, how is Poppa Maddox doing? When is the last time you been to De Motherland?" he asked excitedly, because I barely showed my face unless it was pick-up or drop-off time.

"I went to the slums a few weeks ago to check in on the old man, he's been good. He's been begging to come visit here, so I told him in a few weeks I'll send for him. What about you?" I asked, referring to whether or not he had been to Jamaica.

Me and Kingston went back plenty, out of all my folk, we have always been the closest. I remember back in the day when we would run around the slums with no shoes and were nappy head rug rats. Life was good, we had not a worry in the world.

"Me haven't been back in a while. Me find meself sometimes becoming homesick, but me stay strong for de fam, ya know? A wise man once told I that strength comes in numbers. Everybody ain't as favorable as you are," he said laughing.

"Negro, please, you the man. I respect a man who works for his, not these bumbaclots out here who have their hands out, like a muthafucka owe them something besides a bullet to the dome for disrespecting the game. Any who, excuse me for being a rudeboi. This here is my lady friend, Meeka," I said, introducing them, "and this is my cousin and manager of Glo's, Kingston."

"Nice to meet you," she smiled, placing her hand out to shake his but instead, he brought it to his mouth to kiss.

We walked in the back of the restaurant. I asked Kingston to shut it down today so I could spend a little time with Meeka.

"So, what are we doing?" she asked kindly.

"Well, I thought we could spend some alone time, while you also could show me yo cooking skills. I gotta see if you are wifey material," I said, waiting to see her reaction.

"Alright, we can do that, but don't get mad because I fucked something up."

"Damn, so you can't cook? How you gone try to steal a nigga heart if you can't cook?"

"I guess the same way you expect a nigga to be your servant. It's slim to none." She smiled. "And here I am, getting all dressed up, thinking you want to show me off. I would have even settled for you fucking me with an apron on only."

"Damn ma, like that, huh?"

"I'm just saying." She walked off and I walked up behind her, grabbing her waist and started kissing her neck. I had to stop myself though. I almost forgot where I was. It wasn't the time or place.

"Aight, love, I'ma let you get to it. I hope you know what you doing." I slapped her on that fat ass and walked out.

Meeka

Nigga really had me fucked all the way up, treating me like I was a desperate housewife or some shit? The fuck? I just played along though, because you know a bitch always scheming on a come up, and I know them Jamaican niggas be trying to marry us American hoes for green cards. For whatever reason, my gut was telling me Glo wasn't on that type of kick, but still I was with whatever. I know them crazy muthafuckas knew how to treat a bitch. I mean, queen. It looked like my time had finally come and I was about to bag me a baller, heyy! All in due time.

As I'm preparing this nigga's meal, I had to go way back in my memory bank and pull a couple of recipes my ole grams taught me specially to hook, line and sink a nigga. I whipped up some collard greens, fuck curry chicken. I fried that shit in a flour batter and a little mustard to give it a little tangy taste and the hood all-time favorite Tony's seasoning. My other sides were garlic and butter potatoes, some hot water cornbread and my gram's favorite lemonade.

When I walked to the back where I saw Glo disappear to so I could feed his ass the only way a project bitch could. I damn near dropped the plates. There was someone being held captive. The nigga was being held against his will with his mouth duct taped. *What the fuck this nigga got going on?* I mean, I know he is a hood nigga, but damn! Did he not ever hear to keep his business and pleasure separate? I just shook that shit off though, because I dealt with different niggas on a daily, so it isn't strange for me to run into a face that is familiar. Instead of making my presence known and taking the food to Glo, I stopped, not wanting to interrupt. I decided to eavesdrop instead.

"I'm not understanding why you didn't kill this nigga? What's so hard about doing that? Huh?" Glo asked Kingston.

"Mane, look, didn't want to shoot the whole fucking crowd. There was two chicks out there with him and a kid. Fuck was me supposed to do, knock them off too? You know women and children are off limits."

"With all due respect, cuz, this here game ain't meant for the weak, so if that is what you telling me, then you need to go back home and be a family man. No one is exempt, not even you so get it together, aight?"

That's when they both turned around coming back my way. I ducked back in the kitchen, hoping neither one of them spotted me. My heart began to race because when they turned around, it cleared my path to get a good look at the person sitting in the chair. Killa Kay. *What the fuck was Derrick's homeboy doing here*? These muthafuckas trying to straight MLK niggas. For now though, I was gonna play the game how it go, because momma need a house, baby need shoes and times are getting hard.

Boom.

I flinched. The shot caught me off guard. I knew exactly who that shot was meant for. Glo had just showed Kingston he had no heart and anybody could get it, man, woman or child. Something in my gut told me that the conversation Glo and Kingston was having was sure enough about my baby's father. I didn't know what the fuck to do, because I definitely didn't sign up for a nigga to stop my clock from ticking. Instead of showing any sign of fear, I did what I did best and placed a smile on my face, even when shit wasn't looking good.

Brandon

"Meet me at the spot," I said as soon as D.J. picked up the phone. Ten minutes later, I was pulling up in the projects. I saw his pop's car and knew Derrick might be on some other shit. "Fuck it," I said out loud. I would hate to have to pop his old ass if he get out the box. I hopped out my whip and went straight inside. "What's good, lil sis?" I asked as soon as I saw Beyonca, giving her a tight hug. *I swear, that nigga D.J. take his hoe everywhere*, I thought shaking my head. Maybe one day I'll find love like that, but at the moment the only thing I thought about loving was the money that constantly called my name.

"Nothing much, bro. D.J. in the back waiting on your arrival, with his mean ass daddy."

I entered the basement and saw Derrick sitting at the TV screen, giving it his undivided attention. It looked they were watching the footage from the camera we had set up after the shit happened with my grandmother. I caught a glimpse of it and stopped dead in my tracks.

"The fuck?" I asked myself, walking in the TV's direction. "Rewind that shit and press play, big homie."

"What you notice about that nigga?" Derrick asked as he did what I said.

"Nah, I just know that nigga from somewhere else besides him being a part of Glo's clique, but I can't put my finger on it," I said as we watched the shit unfold before my brother Killa was killed.

I looked over at D.J. for answers. Then it hit me, that nigga worked at that Caribbean joint owned by Glo. Coming up, we used to go cop something to eat back in the day before shit went sour.

"Kingston, I think that's his name, he work for Glo at the restaurant on Lakeside," D.J. said, speaking the words I was thinking.

"So, what's the move, bro? We fucking this nigga whole fam or what?' D. J. asked, always ready to ride.

"That goes without asking, hands down, what you mean? Nigga gone get his. I don't give a fuck bout no fake ass Jamaican Cartel. We bout to show these niggas how us B.R. savages get down."

He knew exactly what time it was.

***

Couple days after we buried my brother, I was ready to cleanse my soul. I felt the need to purge before I lost my fucking mind completely. I began to do drugs and drink, but nothing I consumed deadened the grief I was feeling. The more I dirtied my nose, the more irrational I became.

"Yo, nigga, you need to slow down on that shit, dog. That shit ain't nothing but an invitation to the devil's playground," Derrick said as we sat in my car, watching the nigga Glo and Kingston's restaurant. I didn't comment on the shit this nigga was trying to preach, because I let it go in one ear and out of the other.

"What them niggas in that bitch doing? We been out here on a muthafuckin stakeout for some hours now," D. J. said, becoming vexed with the situation. Fuck! So was I, because I had an itch begging to be scratched.

"There them muthafuckas go right there," I said, getting ready to jump out, until D.J. grabbed my arm.

"What the fuck, nigga?" I asked, looking over at him. "You so-call been waiting on this shit, so what's the fucking probably? You flaking on me, dogg?" I asked, heated.

"Nah, my nigga, nothing about the kid is flaky, but I do want to just sit back just for a second. Let's give them mutha-fuckas time to get from by the building, we don't need they ass running back inside." Damn, I hated to admit it, but D.J. had a good point.

Giving them the time to all come out, I spotted one of our own coming out of that muthafucka.

"You see this pussy ass shit?" I asked them both, becoming even more furious. Now it all made sense. These nigga had the drop on us because Scrappy's dope fiend ass is a trader. I had no fucking understanding.

"Let's go," I said, wishing a muthafucka grabbed me this time.

We all hopped out of the junky rental, pulling the hammers back on our guns and pulling our masks over our faces. These niggas was 'bout to lose their lives and didn't even see the shit coming. It was Kingston, Scrappy and another off-brand ass nigga I had never seen before. I was pissed Glo wasn't here for me to knock that nigga dick in the dirt as well, but for now I'll settle for what I could get.

"Ha, ha, ha, mon that shet was crazy, me going to run de shet by Glo de next time me see de boi."

"I doubt that, my nigga," I said, catching them all off guard.

Boom. Boom. Boom.

With no questions asked, I had just laid the nigga down who was talking, letting those words be his last. I didn't know exactly if he had something to do with the death of Killa Kay, but whether he did or not, he was guilty by association. This is only the beginning of the mayhem I planned to dish out. One pussy nigga down and a few pussy niggas to go.

Boom. Boom. Boom.

Derrick and D.J. followed behind me, knocking Kingston's head off his shoulders, and only wounding Scrappy.

"Please don't kill me! I don't know these niggas like that! I only came to cop some dope, that's it. Mane, I got kids and a girl at home, bruh." Lies continued to flow from his mouth. I walked up on his ass while he laid out on the ground, crying like a little bitch.

"Nigga, stop lying, you ain't got no kids or no muthafuckin girl." I stood over his bitch ass, revealing my face. His eyes popped open as wide as they could go, like he had seen the devil in the flesh. And if I was honest with myself, I would admit that is exactly who I had become in that instant.

"Please, B. I'm sorry, mane." He cried even harder as if his tears moved me.

Boom.

That was the only response I had for his stupid ass. He had to have hit some good shit if he thought I was gone let him live to talk about it. I remember as a lil boy how my family always looked out for his no-good ass. Feeding him when his own momma had thrown him out on his ass. I shook my head. *May my grandma rest in peace.* She was too good for this cold-blooded ass world. I could hear police sirens in the distance and knew we had to go, but I took my chances by placing my latex-gloved hand on each of their necks to check for a pulse.

Good. There was none, but just for great measure, I blessed them niggas with another bullet each to the face. Too many niggas out here taking too many penitentiary chances from leaving niggas behind to tell the story. *No witness, no case.* I lived by that shit and wasn't about to neglect my belief because a nigga was from my neck of the woods. The nigga could have been raised and fed under the same roof, but when you not cut from the same cloth as me or have the same life values, then somebody had to go. That's one of the reasons I was able to walk away with no remorse. There would definitely be no reconstruction of the face for an open casket. I wanted them niggas' families to be just as devastated as mine had been from our loss. In the distance, I could hear the cops closing in on us.

"We gotta go, my nigga," Derrick said as he started walking backwards.

Before I jetted though, I still had unfinished business. I walked over with haste and snatched off Kingston's chain. It will be a token for my family. As long as I lived and let the sunshine upon my face. I'ma wear this nigga's chain until someone feels bold enough to kill me and take it, but it'll have to be over my dead body. As I ran in the direction we had come from, I saw D.J. pull up in Killa's car. I hopped in the front seat as he deserted the premises. While we drove off into the night, I glanced at the picture of my brother and his two daughters, and knew my nigga was proud of me.

Yolanda Moore

Glo

The day I got the disturbing news about my cousin Kingston, I was sitting with my father, having his favorite curry goat, rice and peas and mango juice. I had finally granted his request and brought him to my new home to show him how I was living.

"Excuse me, baby, you have an important call. Would you like to take it in here or should I wait until you finish eating?" Meeka asked.

I had done everything but actually move her things in my home. When I tell you that gal got a gold mine between her legs, and the head she carried on her shoulders, I wish I could cut it off and take it with me.

"Yeah, bring it to me, and could you put some better clothes on that is more appropriate? My father's here," I said, raising my hand to point towards my father.

That was the only thing I didn't like about her. It was one thing to be all freaky and shit with me, but to have her shit hanging out for anybody and everybody with eyes to see, didn't sit well with me. I constantly had to inform her this wasn't the raggedy ass projects she called home. Once she brought me the phone, she went back upstairs to put some fucking clothes on.

"Speak," I said, waiting on the caller to announce who they were.

"Speak? Nigga, you serious? So, you really over there answering the phone like you a king, huh? Well, bitch, you might be the king of Jamaica but on this side of the world, we do shit a little different. It's only enough room for one ruler and it ain't you, bitch."

"Nigga, get off my line with that hoe ass shit you hollin. We getting money over here and don't have much time to hold conversations on the phone like some lil hoes," I said, getting ready to hang up.

"You might want to check out the flick I just sent, nigga," the voice laughed like I had just told a joke, hanging up in my face.

I started not to entertain them bitch ass niggas from the projects, but something told me I should. For one I was clueless on how the fuck this nigga would get my fucking number. As I opened my messages, sure enough there was an icon, indicating I had an attachment to the message. When I opened it, there a picture of Kingston's chain that he wore faithfully and never took off his neck. My uncle, his father, gave it to him before he died, so I knew how much it meant to him.

"G'wan?" my father asked me, reading my sudden silence and facial expression. I was at a loss for words. These bitch ass niggas had finally caught me slipping.

"Baby, are you ok?" Meeka asked me as she rubbed my shoulders.

I disregarded both of the questions that had been thrown at me. I was stuck at the knowledge that nigga had just hit me with, as if I had just been in a head-on collision.

"Baby, answer me," Meeka said again, reviving me from my worst nightmare. I looked up at her with this demonic look in my eyes and a crooked smile on my face.

"No. I'm not ok, but I will be soon, and you are going to make that happen. Understand?"

Six Months Later

Derrion

"Hey, Derrion, how are you?" I heard someone call out to me. I turned around to see Meeka standing beside an all-pink 2021 baby Benz. *Damn, my daddy's baby momma doing it big.* I heard she had been doing good and her standing here in the flesh was enough reason to believe she is doing exactly what the streets are saying.

"I'm ok, girl, what about yourself?" I asked but could clearly see with my own eyes.

"You know, tryna get my shit together like everyone else."

"You look like you doing good, girl," I said, smiling as we both grew quiet. I wondered if she wanted to ask me about my pops because if she did, I really didn't have much to say. I don't get in any of his affairs and don't plan to either.

Before we both could say anything to each other, I heard a baby's cry come from the back seat and for the first time, I noticed a car seat in the back of the car.

"Is that..." I began but was too afraid to finish my sentence. The night Desire ran out of the hospital all hysterical was the night I found out there was a possibility I might have another sibling. But I was too apprehensive to ask my dad if it was true.

"Yeah, you have a little sister. You want to meet her?" she asked, waving her hand, motioning me to approach.

"She's so beautiful," I said, all teary-eyed for many reasons.

The first reason, I was no longer my father's baby girl and the second, she hadn't even had the chance to meet our dad. A tear rolled down my face without warning. I swiftly swiped it away.

"Would you like to come by the house to spend a little time with her? I will have you back home for dinner, I promise," Meeka said as she smiled genuinely.

"Yeah, let me call my dad right quick," I said, taking my phone out.

"No!" she yelled. "I mean, he won't be ok with that. I haven't talked to him since the night Desire found out he was her daddy," Meeka said with fear written across her face.

At first, I was hesitant because of everything that had been going on with my dad and D.J. I didn't know exactly what it was they had gotten themselves into, but I knew it was serious enough for my dad to want to keep up with every move I made.

"Alright, let's go," I smiled as I got in the back seat with my sister.

As we pulled off into traffic, something in my gut told me to follow my first mind, especially the way Meeka kept looking in the rearview mirror. It kinda spooked me out so I discreetly pulled my phone from my pocket and sent my father a text message, letting him know who I was with and where I was going, even though I didn't know the exact location.

Ms. Ethel May Barringer

See, God don't like ugly and He ain't too fond of pretty either,
I thought as I toked on my weed, tapping my feet to the hymn,
"Oh Happy Day." See the thing is, I have a lot to be happy for,
even though them no-good nappy head, pant sagging thugs did
kill my one and only child. Like I said, God doesn't like ugly,
and He sits high and looks low. Every mother knows their
child and for the ones who don't, ain't doing their job.

Before the devil came and snatched my child straight off
the pew in the church house, he had been the God-fearing man
that the Almighty wanted us to be. Walking in his image and
likeness you see. That was before he started fondling with that
hussy, Candy, Meeka's no-good momma and started smoking
that crack. She had my child running around these ole projects
like a chicken with his neck cut off. Like I said, you should
know your child and from the moment they began to spit on
God's good name, I knew my baby boy would never be the
same.

The things he did shamefully on earth I know had his
daddy, my loving husband, turning flips in his final resting
place. But won't He do it? My good faithful God did the hon-
ors and called my baby home, and I was ok with that, even
though I wasn't too fond of the way them dogs just left my
child laid out in the streets like a piece of trash. When I got
the news, I was devastated and that is putting it lightly. I
slammed the door in that white devil's face and hit my knees,
praying for my son's soul. By the time I got out of that position, I could barely walk on these here old knees of mine, but
I was satisfied.

God had promised me that if I ask, I shall receive and with
that said, I was ok with the circumstances of my child, because
he was safe. As for the other hoodlums of these here old

projects, they have been up to their same wicked ways as if the life they are living is what the American dream is all about. But to me, the dream is all about freedom, and I thought someone needed to tap them knuckleheads on the shoulder and tell them it's not in a prison cell. Which is exactly where they were going to end up if they didn't change from their unholy corruption.

After Brandon's brother, Killa Kay, got killed and their poor grandmother, Ms. Chainy, that young man Brandon hadn't been right since. *I feel sorry for him*, I thought, shaking my head. I could only do what's right and that was to keep that child in my prayers, even though the rumor is he was the one responsible for Scrappy's death. I didn't hate him though. I just used him as a steppingstone. Wasn't gone fool around and miss my blessing, all because of their senseless action, no way.

As for Brandon's best friend and partner in crime, D.J., I felt he was the better of the two and definitely wasn't the bad apple of the bunch. I had to admit it I don't know how, because that father of his was just as street and gangsta as they come. At least that's what he thinks, but if he could stop dipping and dabbing in the cookie jar, he might have held on to that sweet girl Desire. I could honestly say though it was his loss and her gain.

I hear through the grapevine that child was living the life, getting ready to have a baby and had gotten married to a doctor. In my honest opinion? She will be back. It was a coincidence she was pregnant that fast for that new husband of hers. I would bet my last rolled-up joint she wasn't even sure who the daddy was. The projects had that type of effect on people, whether you were born and raised here or just passing through, it had a way of sucking you in and keeping a tight grip. Why you think I'm still here?

Meeka, Meeka, Meeka. I had to shake my head at the child. If it wasn't for her being the spitting image of my son, Scrappy, I would have denied her butt a long time ago. I remember the day her no-good momma dropped her off on my porch and didn't even have the courtesy to even look back. Nobody actually knew Meeka was my grandchild. It was something I dared not speak on. Not because I was ashamed, but because I just didn't like inviting folks in my business. That was just the way I was brought up, to never put yo business out in the streets. Any who, in more than one way, Meeka was just like my son. And it was a shame too. I just prayed the repeated cycle would change. Hopefully, the next generation would get it together and change the world maybe.

My mind and heart all of a sudden got weary and went out to that child, Keisha. A few months ago, her daughter was shot, missing death by the skin of her teeth. I rejoiced when I heard that child had faced off with the devil and beat him at his own game. But it is apparent my prayers wasn't enough, because a couple of weeks ago baby Derrick, for the sake of the Lord I couldn't recall that child's name, so I settled with calling her baby Derrick. Any who, as I was saying, a few weeks ago that child disappeared, and no one has heard from her since. The streets are saying that granddaughter of mine had something to do with it, but that's neither here nor there. As I said so many times, the apple doesn't fall too far from the tree.

"Hey, Ms. Ethel, how are you?"

"Oh chile, these here old bones are crumbling right from under me, but the Lord has been good to me so I can't complain," I said, waving at Pastor John's child, Jo Jo. *I bet his fast tail had a good ole time locked behind bars with them perverted men*, I thought still smiling politely as he passed on by.

I continued on with the hymn, "Oh Happy Day," as the sun shined upon my face. I didn't have a worry in the world as I smoked my weed, slowly drifting into another world. The pain that had once taken over my body, had begun to linger and then suddenly left my body, as I drifted into the bright light shining upon my face. If I didn't know any better, I would have thought the good ole Lord was calling me home. Maybe he was and if that is the case, I wouldn't be mad either. I had seen all I needed on this earth and truth be told, I was ready to leave and be reunited with my one true love.

Ms. Ethel May Barringer
1935-2021

To Be Continued...
The Streets Will Talk 2
Coming Soon

Lock Down Publications and Ca$h Presents assisted publishing packages.

BASIC PACKAGE $499
Editing
Cover Design
Formatting

UPGRADED PACKAGE $800
Typing
Editing
Cover Design
Formatting

ADVANCE PACKAGE $1,200
Typing
Editing
Cover Design
Formatting
Copyright registration
Proofreading
Upload book to Amazon

LDP SUPREME PACKAGE $1,500
Typing
Editing
Cover Design
Formatting
Copyright registration
Proofreading
Set up Amazon account
Upload book to Amazon

Yolanda Moore

Advertise on LDP Amazon and Facebook page

***Other services available upon request. Additional charges may apply
Lock Down Publications
P.O. Box 944
Stockbridge, GA 30281-9998
Phone # 470 303-9761

Submission Guideline

Submit the first three chapters of your completed manuscript to ldpsubmissions@gmail.com, subject line: Your book's title. The manuscript must be in a .doc file and sent as an attachment. Document should be in Times New Roman, double spaced and in size 12 font. Also, provide your synopsis and full contact information. If sending multiple submissions, they must each be in a separate email.

Have a story but no way to send it electronically? You can still submit to LDP/Ca$h Presents. Send in the first three chapters, written or typed, of your completed manuscript to:

LDP: Submissions Dept
Po Box 944
Stockbridge, Ga 30281

DO NOT send original manuscript. Must be a duplicate.

Provide your synopsis and a cover letter containing your full contact information.

Thanks for considering LDP and Ca$h Presents.

<u>NEW RELEASES</u>

SAVAGE STORMS 3 by MEESHA
LOYAL TO THE SOIL 3 by JIBRIL WILLIAMS
THE STREETS WILL NEVER CLOSE by K'AJJI
MONEY IN THE GRAVE 3 by MARTELL "TROUBLE-
SOME" BOLDEN
BETRAYAL OF A THUG by FRE$H
THE STREETS WILL TALK by YOLANDA MOORE

Coming Soon from Lock Down Publications/Ca$h Presents

BLOOD OF A BOSS VI

SHADOWS OF THE GAME II

TRAP BASTARD II

By **Askari**

LOYAL TO THE GAME IV

By **T.J. & Jelissa**

IF TRUE SAVAGE VIII

MIDNIGHT CARTEL IV

DOPE BOY MAGIC IV

CITY OF KINGZ III

NIGHTMARE ON SILENT AVE II

THE PLUG OF LIL MEXICO II

By **Chris Green**

BLAST FOR ME III

A SAVAGE DOPEBOY III

CUTTHROAT MAFIA III

DUFFLE BAG CARTEL VII

HEARTLESS GOON VI

By **Ghost**

A HUSTLER'S DECEIT III

KILL ZONE II

BAE BELONGS TO ME III

By **Aryanna**

KING OF THE TRAP III

By **T.J. Edwards**

GORILLAZ IN THE BAY V

3X KRAZY III

STRAIGHT BEAST MODE II

De'Kari

KINGPIN KILLAZ IV

STREET KINGS III

PAID IN BLOOD III

CARTEL KILLAZ IV

DOPE GODS III

Hood Rich

SINS OF A HUSTLA II

ASAD

RICH $AVAGE II

By Martell Troublesome Bolden

YAYO V

Bred In The Game 2

S. Allen

CREAM III

THE STREETS WILL TALK II

By Yolanda Moore

SON OF A DOPE FIEND III

HEAVEN GOT A GHETTO II

By Renta

LOYALTY AIN'T PROMISED III

By Keith Williams

I'M NOTHING WITHOUT HIS LOVE II

SINS OF A THUG II

TO THE THUG I LOVED BEFORE II

The Street Will Talk

IN A HUSTLER I TRUST II
By Monet Dragun
QUIET MONEY IV
EXTENDED CLIP III
THUG LIFE IV
By **Trai'Quan**
THE STREETS MADE ME IV
By **Larry D. Wright**
IF YOU CROSS ME ONCE II
By **Anthony Fields**
THE STREETS WILL NEVER CLOSE III
By K'ajji
HARD AND RUTHLESS III
THE BILLIONAIRE BENTLEYS III
Von Diesel
KILLA KOUNTY III
By Khufu
MONEY GAME III
By Smoove Dolla
JACK BOYS VS DOPE BOYS II
A GANGSTA'S QUR'AN V
By Romell Tukes
MURDA WAS THE CASE II
Elijah R. Freeman
THE STREETS NEVER LET GO II
By Robert Baptiste
AN UNFORESEEN LOVE III

175

Yolanda Moore

By **Meesha**

KING OF THE TRENCHES III
by **GHOST & TRANAY ADAMS**

MONEY MAFIA II

LOYAL TO THE SOIL III

By **Jibril Williams**

QUEEN OF THE ZOO II

By **Black Migo**

THE BRICK MAN IV

THE COCAINE PRINCESS III

By King Rio

VICIOUS LOYALTY II

By Kingpen

A GANGSTA'S PAIN II

By J-Blunt

CONFESSIONS OF A JACKBOY III

By Nicholas Lock

GRIMEY WAYS II

By Ray Vinci

KING KILLA II

By Vincent "Vitto" Holloway

BETRAYAL OF A THUG II

By Fre$h

Available Now

RESTRAINING ORDER **I & II**

By **CA$H & Coffee**

LOVE KNOWS NO BOUNDARIES **I II & III**

By **Coffee**

RAISED AS A GOON I, II, III & IV

BRED BY THE SLUMS I, II, III

BLAST FOR ME I & II

ROTTEN TO THE CORE I II III

A BRONX TALE I, II, III

DUFFLE BAG CARTEL I II III IV V VI

HEARTLESS GOON I II III IV V

A SAVAGE DOPEBOY I II

DRUG LORDS I II III

CUTTHROAT MAFIA I II

KING OF THE TRENCHES

By **Ghost**

LAY IT DOWN **I & II**

LAST OF A DYING BREED I II

BLOOD STAINS OF A SHOTTA I & II III

By **Jamaica**

LOYAL TO THE GAME I II III

LIFE OF SIN I, II III

By **TJ & Jelissa**

BLOODY COMMAS I & II

SKI MASK CARTEL I II & III

KING OF NEW YORK I II,III IV V

RISE TO POWER I II III

COKE KINGS I II III IV V

BORN HEARTLESS I II III IV

KING OF THE TRAP I II

By **T.J. Edwards**

IF LOVING HIM IS WRONG…I & II

LOVE ME EVEN WHEN IT HURTS I II III

By **Jelissa**

WHEN THE STREETS CLAP BACK I & II III

THE HEART OF A SAVAGE I II III

MONEY MAFIA

LOYAL TO THE SOIL I II

By **Jibril Williams**

A DISTINGUISHED THUG STOLE MY HEART I II & III

LOVE SHOULDN'T HURT I II III IV

RENEGADE BOYS I II III IV

PAID IN KARMA I II III

SAVAGE STORMS I II III

AN UNFORESEEN LOVE I II

By **Meesha**

A GANGSTER'S CODE I &, II III

A GANGSTER'S SYN I II III

THE SAVAGE LIFE I II III

The Street Will Talk

CHAINED TO THE STREETS I II III
BLOOD ON THE MONEY I II III
A GANGSTA'S PAIN
By J-Blunt
PUSH IT TO THE LIMIT
By **Bre' Hayes**
BLOOD OF A BOSS **I, II, III, IV, V**
SHADOWS OF THE GAME
TRAP BASTARD
By **Askari**
THE STREETS BLEED MURDER **I, II & III**
THE HEART OF A GANGSTA I II& III
By **Jerry Jackson**
CUM FOR ME I II III IV V VI VII VIII
An **LDP Erotica Collaboration**
BRIDE OF A HUSTLA **I II & II**
THE FETTI GIRLS **I, II& III**
CORRUPTED BY A GANGSTA I, II III, IV
BLINDED BY HIS LOVE
THE PRICE YOU PAY FOR LOVE I, II ,III
DOPE GIRL MAGIC I II III
By **Destiny Skai**
WHEN A GOOD GIRL GOES BAD
By **Adrienne**
THE COST OF LOYALTY I II III
By Kweli
A GANGSTER'S REVENGE **I II III & IV**

Yolanda Moore

THE BOSS MAN'S DAUGHTERS I II III IV V

A SAVAGE LOVE **I & II**

BAE BELONGS TO ME I II

A HUSTLER'S DECEIT I, II, III

WHAT BAD BITCHES DO I, II, III

SOUL OF A MONSTER I II III

KILL ZONE

A DOPE BOY'S QUEEN I II III

By **Aryanna**

A KINGPIN'S AMBITON

A KINGPIN'S AMBITION **II**

I MURDER FOR THE DOUGH

By **Ambitious**

TRUE SAVAGE I II III IV V VI VII

DOPE BOY MAGIC I, II, III

MIDNIGHT CARTEL I II III

CITY OF KINGZ I II

NIGHTMARE ON SILENT AVE

THE PLUG OF LIL MEXICO II

By **Chris Green**

A DOPEBOY'S PRAYER

By **Eddie "Wolf" Lee**

THE KING CARTEL **I, II & III**

By **Frank Gresham**

THESE NIGGAS AIN'T LOYAL **I, II & III**

By **Nikki Tee**

180

GANGSTA SHYT **I II &III**

By **CATO**

THE ULTIMATE BETRAYAL

By **Phoenix**

BOSS'N UP **I , II & III**

By **Royal Nicole**

I LOVE YOU TO DEATH

By **Destiny J**

I RIDE FOR MY HITTA

I STILL RIDE FOR MY HITTA

By **Misty Holt**

LOVE & CHASIN' PAPER

By **Qay Crockett**

TO DIE IN VAIN

SINS OF A HUSTLA

By **ASAD**

BROOKLYN HUSTLAZ

By **Boogsy Morina**

BROOKLYN ON LOCK I & II

By **Sonovia**

GANGSTA CITY

By **Teddy Duke**

A DRUG KING AND HIS DIAMOND I & II III

A DOPEMAN'S RICHES

HER MAN, MINE'S TOO I, II

CASH MONEY HO'S

THE WIFEY I USED TO BE I II

Yolanda Moore

By Nicole Goosby

TRAPHOUSE KING **I II & III**

KINGPIN KILLAZ I II III

STREET KINGS I II

PAID IN BLOOD **I II**

CARTEL KILLAZ I II III

DOPE GODS I II

By **Hood Rich**

LIPSTICK KILLAH **I, II, III**

CRIME OF PASSION I II & III

FRIEND OR FOE I II III

By **Mimi**

STEADY MOBBN' **I, II, III**

THE STREETS STAINED MY SOUL I II III

By **Marcellus Allen**

WHO SHOT YA **I, II, III**

SON OF A DOPE FIEND I II

HEAVEN GOT A GHETTO

Renta

GORILLAZ IN THE BAY **I II III IV**

TEARS OF A GANGSTA I II

3X KRAZY I II

STRAIGHT BEAST MODE

DE'KARI

TRIGGADALE I II III

MURDAROBER WAS THE CASE

Elijah R. Freeman

182

GOD BLESS THE TRAPPERS I, II, III

THESE SCANDALOUS STREETS I, II, III

FEAR MY GANGSTA I, II, III IV, V

THESE STREETS DON'T LOVE NOBODY I, II

BURY ME A G I, II, III, IV, V

A GANGSTA'S EMPIRE I, II, III, IV

THE DOPEMAN'S BODYGAURD I II

THE REALEST KILLAZ I II III

THE LAST OF THE OGS I II III

Tranay Adams

THE STREETS ARE CALLING

Duquie Wilson

MARRIED TO A BOSS I II III

By Destiny Skai & Chris Green

KINGZ OF THE GAME I II III IV V VI

Playa Ray

SLAUGHTER GANG I II III

RUTHLESS HEART I II III

By Willie Slaughter

FUK SHYT

By Blakk Diamond

DON'T F#CK WITH MY HEART I II

By Linnea

ADDICTED TO THE DRAMA I II III

IN THE ARM OF HIS BOSS II

By Jamila

YAYO I II III IV

Yolanda Moore

A SHOOTER'S AMBITION I II

BRED IN THE GAME

By S. Allen

TRAP GOD I II III

RICH $AVAGE

MONEY IN THE GRAVE I II III

By Martell Troublesome Bolden

FOREVER GANGSTA

GLOCKS ON SATIN SHEETS I II

By Adrian Dulan

TOE TAGZ I II III IV

LEVELS TO THIS SHYT I II

By Ah'Million

KINGPIN DREAMS I II III

By Paper Boi Rari

CONFESSIONS OF A GANGSTA I II III IV

CONFESSIONS OF A JACKBOY I II

By Nicholas Lock

I'M NOTHING WITHOUT HIS LOVE

SINS OF A THUG

TO THE THUG I LOVED BEFORE

A GANGSTA SAVED XMAS

IN A HUSTLER I TRUST

By Monet Dragun

CAUGHT UP IN THE LIFE I II III

THE STREETS NEVER LET GO

By Robert Baptiste

NEW TO THE GAME I II III

MONEY, MURDER & MEMORIES I II III

By **Malik D. Rice**

LIFE OF A SAVAGE I II III

A GANGSTA'S QUR'AN I II III IV

MURDA SEASON I II III

GANGLAND CARTEL I II III

CHI'RAQ GANGSTAS I II III

KILLERS ON ELM STREET I II III

JACK BOYZ N DA BRONX I II III

A DOPEBOY'S DREAM I II III

JACK BOYS VS DOPE BOYS

By **Romell Tukes**

LOYALTY AIN'T PROMISED I II

By Keith Williams

QUIET MONEY I II III

THUG LIFE I II III

EXTENDED CLIP I II

By **Trai'Quan**

THE STREETS MADE ME I II III

By **Larry D. Wright**

THE ULTIMATE SACRIFICE I, II, III, IV, V, VI

KHADIFI

IF YOU CROSS ME ONCE

ANGEL I II

IN THE BLINK OF AN EYE

By **Anthony Fields**

Yolanda Moore

THE LIFE OF A HOOD STAR
By Ca$h & Rashia Wilson
THE STREETS WILL NEVER CLOSE I II
By K'ajji
CREAM I II
THE STREETS WILL TALK
By Yolanda Moore
NIGHTMARES OF A HUSTLA I II III
By King Dream
CONCRETE KILLA I II
VICIOUS LOYALTY
By Kingpen
HARD AND RUTHLESS I II
MOB TOWN 251
THE BILLIONAIRE BENTLEYS I II
By Von Diesel
GHOST MOB
Stilloan Robinson
MOB TIES I II III IV V
By SayNoMore
BODYMORE MURDERLAND I II III
By Delmont Player
FOR THE LOVE OF A BOSS
By C. D. Blue
MOBBED UP I II III IV
THE BRICK MAN I II III
THE COCAINE PRINCESS I II

186

The Street Will Talk

By King Rio
KILLA KOUNTY I II
By Khufu
MONEY GAME I II
By Smoove Dolla
A GANGSTA'S KARMA I II
By FLAME
KING OF THE TRENCHES I II
by **GHOST & TRANAY ADAMS**
QUEEN OF THE ZOO
By **Black Migo**
GRIMEY WAYS
By Ray Vinci
XMAS WITH AN ATL SHOOTER
By Ca$h & Destiny Skai
KING KILLA
By Vincent "Vitto" Holloway
BETRAYAL OF A THUG
By Fre$h

Yolanda Moore

<u>BOOKS BY LDP'S CEO, CA$H</u>

TRUST IN NO MAN

TRUST IN NO MAN 2

TRUST IN NO MAN 3

BONDED BY BLOOD

SHORTY GOT A THUG

THUGS CRY

THUGS CRY 2

THUGS CRY 3

TRUST NO BITCH

TRUST NO BITCH 2

TRUST NO BITCH 3

TIL MY CASKET DROPS

RESTRAINING ORDER

RESTRAINING ORDER 2

IN LOVE WITH A CONVICT

LIFE OF A HOOD STAR

XMAS WITH AN ATL SHOOTER

The Street Will Talk

www.ingramcontent.com/pod-product-compliance
Lightning Source LLC
Chambersburg PA
CBHW070518260626
47161CB00004B/1583